REFLECTION
OF A
KILLER

REFLECTION OF A KILLER

Published by
ShahrazaD Publishing®
2189 W Canyon Court
Grand Junction, CO 81507-2574

Library of Congress Control Number: 2021917740

ISBN – 9781685243234

Contact the authors at:
judyblevins@bresnan.net
carrollmultz@charter.net

ALSO BY THE AUTHORS

Novels

By Judith Blevins

Double Jeopardy • *Swan Song*
Legacy • *Karma* • *Paragon*

By Carroll Multz

Justice Denied • *Deadly Deception* • *License to Convict*
The Devil's Scribe • *The Chameleon*
Shades of Innocence • *The Winning Ticket*

By Judith Blevins & Carroll Multz

Rogue Justice • *The Plagiarist* • *A Desperate Plea*
Spiderweb • *The Méjico Connection*
Eyewitness • *Lust for Revenge* • *Kamanda* • *Bloodline*
Pickpocket • *Ghost Writer* • *Guilt by Innuendo*
Gypsy Card Reader • *Waves of Vengeance*
Veil of Deceit • *The Journalist* • *We the Jury*
Star Chamber

Childhood Legends Series®
By Judith Blevins & Carroll Multz

Operation Cat Tale • *One Frightful Day* • *Blue*
The Ghost of Bradbury Mansion • *White Out*
Flash of Red • *Back in Time* • *Treasure Seekers*
Summer Vacation-Part 1: Castaways-Part 2: Blast Off
*A Trip to Remember —The R*U*1*2s Journey*
to the Nation's Capital

Dedication

To the Incorruptible.

The better part of valor is discretion!

Shakespeare

TABLE OF CONTENTS

A Note From The Authors

*D*on't do as I do, do as I say! *For thee, but not for me!* There are many ways to phrase the subjective standard that rules are made to be followed by everyone except *thine self.*

It appears in our society today that rules (laws) are mandatory for the governed and advisory for those who govern. Power carries with it special privileges and immunities but apparently not the duties and responsibilities relegated to the masses. What happened to the equal treatment of the law guaranteed by our nation's great charter—the United States Constitution? The privileges and immunities were meant to be applied equally regardless of race, color, creed, or status.

All is fair in love, war, and politics — at least according to our antagonist in the novel you are about to read. Should fairness ever be based on a person's race, color, creed or social, economic, or political status. Your authors are reminded of *Kant's Categorical Imperative: What would happen if everyone did what I'm contemplating doing or didn't do what I'm contemplating not doing? Would the world be better off* or *worse off?* Ponder it as you read through the pages of our latest novel,

Reflection of a Killer.

Special thanks to Lisa Knudson for her editing skills, Frank Addington, for the cover and interior book designs; and Rosalie Stewart and John Lukon of KC Book Manufacturing for printing *Reflection of a Killer*, and finally, to our readers, you continue to be our inspiration.

Chapter One

Proceed With Caution

The frosted glass window in my office door identifies me as: *Jack Cooper, Private Investigator.* I'm a one-man show. No receptionist, no secretary, no partner, nor do I have a dog. Just me!

When she showed up for her appointment, I knew the minute she walked in that she was trouble. She had *proceed with caution* written all over her. I motioned for her to be seated on one of the chairs in front of my desk and asked, "How can I help you, Mrs. Lexington?"

She took a seat and placed her purse on the floor beside her chair. Then looking at me, she said, "Mr. Cooper, Leonard Lexington is my husband. And as you probably know, he's running for the United States Senate."

"Yes, I do know! However, I try to stay out of politics—"

She was quick to interrupt. "My predicament has nothing to do with politics *per se*. You see, when my problem persisted, I was at wits end and didn't know where else to turn. Then I remembered that some years ago you did some work for a friend of mine. My friend was pleased with the results of your investigation and that's why I came to you."

"That's nice to know. Go on, Mrs. Lexington, what's your problem?"

"Please call me Margot. I much prefer it to Mrs. Lexington," she said pointedly.

"And I prefer Jack to Mr. Cooper. Now…"

"I'm being blackmailed, and I need your help!" she said.

"I see," I said and waited. She appeared to be reluctant to provide details, so when she didn't immediately respond, I encouraged her to continue. "Now, who is it that's blackmailing you and why?"

Margot slid back further into the leather chair and crossed her legs. The stilettos she was wearing enhanced the shapeliness of her long gams and I tried not to gawk. Her demeanor and style reminded me of the Hollywood's golden age when glamorous stars filled the screens in movie houses across the nation. A time when teens, decked out in poodle skirts and bobby socks, zeroed in on celebrities vying with each other just to get an autograph.

Margot reached down and methodically removed a cigarette case from her designer handbag. Holding a cigarette between her fingers, she looked at me expectantly. Since cigarettes had been on the hit list for several years, I no longer had a lighter, or even matches in my office. I pointed to the *No Smoking* plaque positioned on my desk. Glancing at it, she shrugged, replaced the cigarette, and methodically slipped the case back into her purse.

"I don't know who the blackmailer is," she replied. "After receiving the initial blackmail demand, I began receiving messages on my iPhone reminding me when and where a payment was due."

Margot hesitated after each sentence and it appeared that I was going to have to pry all the pertinent information from her, so I asked, "How much are the payments?"

"Five thousand dollars."

"Five thousand dollars! How do you make the *payments* and how often?" I asked.

"Once a month I mail the payment to a post office box. The box number changes every month."

Five-thousand-dollar monthly payments stunned me. *For that kind of money, the information the blackmailer has must be pretty significant.* "What's this blackmailer holding over your head?" I asked.

Margot's face immediately changed expression and contorted with desperation. It was obvious she hadn't expected me to be so blunt and she jerked upright in her chair when I posed the question. I watched her glance at her purse, apparently wishing she could have a smoke. She finally blurted, "About six-months ago I attended a friend's fortieth birthday party. With the number of friends toasting her during the evening, I drank more than I should've. It was dark and rainy when the party broke up. When I left, I didn't feel intoxicated and thought that I was able to drive. I should've known better."

Tears began to slip down Margot's cheeks, and she roughly swiped at them with her fingers as she continued. "I was in a hurry to get home and was driving too fast. In fact, it was raining so hard, the wipers were barely able to keep up with the deluge. As I approached an intersection, I saw something in the headlights and slammed on the brakes. The car went into a skid, and I heard a thump as something hit the right front fender."

When she paused, I prompted her to continue, "Then what?"

Her eyes clouded with tears and anxiety was apparent in her voice as she whispered, "I panicked and sped away. I thought I had hit a large dog. Because of the heavy downpour and having drank too much alcohol at the party, I didn't stop to investigate. I didn't know until the next day when I read about the accident in the newspaper that I probably was the driver who hit and killed a teenager. The paper reported that the young man had just left a late movie and was crossing the street when the accident occurred."

I waited a few moments thinking she was taking a breather. When it appeared she was finished, I said, "It's not too late to turn yourself in—"

"No! I can't do that!" Looking forlorn, Margot shifted in her chair. "My grandmother left me a small inheritance which I've almost depleted mainly by making blackmail payments."

I leaned forward and tented my fingers on my desk. Staring at her, I said, "I'm assuming, since you're making the payments from your inheritance, that your husband doesn't know about the accident or the blackmail."

"That's correct," Margot snapped.

Judging by her reaction, I must've hit a nerve. "Why not?"

"Why not? The reason I didn't tell Leonard was because the Senate race is hotly contested, and a scandal of this nature would certainly destroy his chances of winning. Not to mention his ultimate bid for the Whitehouse. I'm fairly confident the opposition would use every scintilla of scandal they could dig up associated with the Lexington name to vilify Leonard in order to sink his ship. I'd do anything to keep that from happening. Being a senator and ultimately president has been Leonard's lifelong dream."

After glancing once again at her purse, she finally said, "When I left the scene, thinking I had hit a dog, I was sure no one witnessed the accident. I obviously wasn't thinking clearly in my drunken stupor, and my first impulse was to get as far away from there as quickly as possible."

I nodded. "And what proof did the blackmailer provide that it was you he saw hit the teen?"

Margot took a deep breath. "Well, the car is registered in my name. I don't suppose that information would be too hard to come by. Since Leonard entered the Senate race, our privacy is almost nonexistent. He was required to file paperwork with the Federal Election Commission and the records are open to the public. I'm assuming that's how the blackmailer got my phone number as well. The blackmailer ah… emailed me a video depicting the victim's body sprawled in the street and the rear ah… of my car with the license plate in plain view speeding from the scene. I ah… immediately destroyed the video for obvious reasons."

Margot slumped in her chair. It appeared that confessing was too much for her, and she began sobbing again. I turned and retrieved a bottle of water from the small frig next to my credenza and offered it to her. Her hand shook as she accepted it.

"Thank you," she whispered.

"You're welcome. Now, what is it you want me to do?"

Margot looked at me as if I'd grown another head. "Isn't it obvious! I want you to find out who the blackmailer is. If I had that information, I could bargain with him—my silence in exchange for his silence."

"Sorry, Mrs. Lexington. You're asking me to be a complicitor involving several crimes, the most serious being vehicular homicide, a felony. Ethically, I cannot do that and morally, I will not! Since your confessing to me could be considered hearsay by the authorities, and you could deny it, I won't file a police report, but my advice is for you—"

"Never mind! I don't want your advice!" Margot shouted. Standing, she tucked the designer handbag under her arm and stormed out of my office slamming the door behind her. That was the last time I saw her alive.

REFLECTION OF A KILLER — JUDITH BLEVINS & CARROLL MULTZ

Chapter Two

A Picture Is Worth
A Thousand Words

It was shortly after the senatorial election that my police scanner alerted me to a death at the Lexington residence. Although I didn't know who the victim was at the time, I thought perhaps my meeting with Margot may be of help to the authorities, especially since I knew there was a blackmailer on the loose and could possibly have been involved in the death. Although I could not divulge the source of my knowledge or betray Margot's trust, I could drop a few helpful hints.

• • •

The Lexington estate, which was located in Denver in the exclusive Cherry Hills area, was cordoned off with police tape. However, when I arrived, the entrance wasn't guarded, so I walked in. Once inside, I noticed a door off the foyer standing open. It appeared to be the door to a study and the county medical examiner, Preston Wheeler, was kneeling beside a body. I glanced around the entryway. No uniforms were present, so since I was still unrestrained by anyone wearing a badge,

I walked in the direction of the open door. When I got close enough, I immediately recognized the victim as Margot Lexington. Wheeler, apparently absorbed in his examination, didn't look up when I approached. I squatted beside him, "How long's she been dead?" I asked.

"Oh, I'd say approximately eight hours," he replied. He apparently didn't immediately realize I was not authorized personnel.

"Cause of death?" I asked.

Before answering, Wheeler removed his glasses, and looking up, gave me a disapproving glance. It was then it must've occurred to him that I was an interloper. Sitting back on his haunches with a disgusted expression on his face, he exclaimed, "Hey, Cooper, aren't you overstepping your bounds?" Looking back over his shoulder toward the entrance, he quired, "How'd you get in here without an official pass?"

I rose to my feet and answered, "Through that door over there," and pointed to the expensive, oversized, oak door that separated the study from the rest of the expensive, oversized, fifteen-room mansion.

"For cryin' out loud! You of all people should know better than to contaminate a crime scene with your unauthorized presence. Just take yourself right back out of *that door over there,"* Wheeler remarked as he pointed to the open door and looked at me as if daring me to challenge him. When I didn't make a move to leave, he grumbled something inaudible and turned back to conducting his cursory postmortem examination.

"I know the vic," I said. "She recently engaged my services—"

Looking up again, Wheeler replied, "Be that as it may, you shouldn't be here, and I can't—"

"I know that, and I don't want to put you on the spot, but is there anything you can tell me?" I asked.

Again, sitting back on his haunches, Wheeler paused and rubbed the back of his neck, "Only that it appears she was shot in the chest… and you didn't hear it from me," he cautioned. He then asked, "What did she need with a PI?"

Before I could respond, two men barged into the room. They were instantly irate upon spotting me. I recognized them as Denver Police detectives Russel Thornton and Finn Doyle.

Advancing toward us, Thornton shouted, "Hey! What the hell's Jack Cooper doing in here?"

Without looking up from the body, Wheeler stammered, "I donno. Thought you gave him the go ahead."

Glaring at Wheeler, Thornton rebuffed, "Not

likely! Since when are PIs allowed to view crime scenes even before the CSIs arrive?" Then turning to me, he ordered, "Get outta here right now before I throw your ass in the can for trespassing and compromising a crime scene."

Thornton's a good cop, but his social skills are nonexistent. I know when I'm not wanted so I immediately vacated the premises.

• • •

Back in my office, I pulled the Lexington file and began searching through my notes hoping to find something that would point to who the killer might be. I discounted the blackmailer as a possibility. Five thousand bucks a month ain't nothin' to sneeze at so why kill the goose that laid the golden egg. I wondered if Leonard could have made some enemies because of his political aspirations and perhaps was the intended victim, not Margot.

Even though I didn't take on her case, my meeting with Margot piqued my interest in the Lexingtons. I therefore made it a practice to clip all the newspaper accounts concerning Leonard Lexington and his campaign for senator and watched the onslaught of newscasts as the November election date drew near. I thought perhaps I could fit the pieces together and thus figure out who the blackmailer was. I closely studied the articles and newspaper photographs of those attending the campaign rallies, and using a magnifying glass, I examined the faces and matched them with the names listed in the articles. One face in particular grabbed my attention. The woman in the photograph looked exactly like Margot. However, in this photo, it was obvious that Margot was standing next to her husband, so it couldn't have been her. I found out by reading the article that the lookalike was Paige Fontaine.

The Internet carried bios of the Lexingtons and I soon discovered Paige Fontaine was Margot's sister. She was two years older than Margot, never married, graduated from Duke University, and currently resided in Savannah, Georgia.

• • •

A week later, after the ME finished conducting the postmortem and gathering forensic evidence from the body, Margot's remains were released for burial. I attended the funeral and took a position in the last pew where I could view those in attendance. I knew it was a longshot, but if the blackmailer showed up, perhaps he would tip his hand.

A month before Margot's death, Leonard had been elected and was now a United States senator. Margot's funeral was attended not only by family and friends, but by many other elected officials. The newly elected senator was ensconced between other members of the Lexington family. However, I thought it odd that the person I recognized as Margot's sister, Paige Fontaine, sat outside the area designated for family members. Her face was somewhat hidden behind a black veil, and it was obvious she was overcome with grief. She constantly reached beneath the veil and dabbed at her eyes with a handkerchief. Occasionally I observed her shoulders shake apparently from sobbing over the loss of her sister.

At the conclusion of the service, since I was close to the exit of the church, I made a hasty and hopefully unobserved getaway and drove immediately to the cemetery. Once there, I selected a vantage point where I could watch the mourners. Paige arrived by taxi, and I thought it odd that none of the family would drive her to the cemetery. The graveside service was short, and Paige remained at the burial site long after everyone had left. I stayed out of sight not wanting to intrude on her solitude. When she finally stood and turned, apparently preparing to leave, I approached her.

"Ms. Fontaine," I said, "I'm Jack Cooper—"

Paige had removed the veil and looked at me with red, swollen eyes. I was surprised when she said, "Yes, I know who you are. I saw you at the funeral. Margot told me about her meeting with you and she did a pretty good job of describing you."

Not knowing what Margot may have told Paige after she abruptly stormed from my office, and not sure if Paige was friend or foe, I chose my words carefully. "My condolences at your loss," I said in a quiet voice as I walked alongside her.

"Thank you…" Paige said in a similar tone.

The way her voice trailed off, I got the impression she wanted to say more, so I took a chance and said, "I see you have a taxi waiting. However, I'd like to talk to you. May I offer you a ride back to your hotel?"

Glancing at the waiting taxi, Paige answered, "I'd like that. I was hoping to meet with you before I went back to Savannah."

I paid the cab driver, dismissed him, and escorted Paige to my vehicle. Once we were clear of the cemetery, I said, "We could stop somewhere and have coffee if you like."

"Yes, that would be nice. My throat seems to be parched."

It was mid-afternoon and *Blair's Coffee House* was almost devoid of patrons when we entered. After we were served, I began the conversation. "Some time ago your sister came to me wanting me to do some investigating for her—"

"I know," Paige interrupted, "she told me about it. I know what she told you at that meeting and would like your take on the conversation if you're at liberty to discuss it with me. Margot and I shared everything even though we lived a great distance apart. We always had each other's back, even in grammar school. We were as close as two sisters could be."

"I see. And what did she tell you?" I asked still uncertain if Paige was friend or foe.

"First of all, Mr. Cooper, she admitted to me that she acted impulsively when she stormed from your office and that she later regretted it," Paige said in a soft voice. "However, Margot's pride kept her from calling you and apologizing."

"Please call me Jack and thank you for putting my mind at ease. I, too, had misgivings, and in retrospect, I believe I could've handled my end of the situation a lot differently."

Paige nodded. "I knew my sister well enough to know she would want me to reveal what I'm about to tell you." Pausing, Paige gently swirled the stir stick around in her coffee cup, apparently buying time as she searched for the right words. She finally said, "Leonard was driving Margot's car the night the teen was hit and killed! It was *he* who killed the teen—not Margot."

After the spiel Margot had laid on me when we met, that came as a shock. "The senator was driving?" I asked—as an exclamation as much as a question.

"That's correct," Paige said and looked around apparently hoping no one had overheard me. No one seemed to be paying attention to us, so she continued. "The fear was that, if the authorities traced the accident back to him, Leonard's political career would be over. Margot told me she never left the house the night of the accident and wasn't present when the accident occurred. She said Leonard had borrowed her car because his was low on gas and he was afraid he'd run out and be stranded."

Lowering her voice in a conspiratorial whisper, she continued, "Then, in order to cover his own ass if an investigation ended up on their doorstep after the accident, the rat-bastard coerced Margot into agreeing to take the blame to save his political career, even to the point of letting her know he would *make her life miserable* if she didn't. Then when the blackmailer reared his ugly head zeroing in on Margot, not Leonard, that pretty much sealed her fate."

Still reeling from the revelation that the senator

was driving that fateful night, I asked, "Did she tell you what make *her life miserable* meant?"

"Didn't have to. We both knew what that meant," Paige answered in a barely audible voice. "Leonard may come across as a sweet, loveable guy, but he has a sinister black heart. He's a controller and a verbal abuser. He wouldn't dare leave marks on her that would verify that his constant correcting, criticizing, chiding, and verbal abuse amounted to domestic violence. Although some of his abusive language was done in public and in front of their friends, he for the most part kept secret his demoniac side. She told me she got to the place where she was afraid to say anything. He was the master at turning nothing into a major incident if it made him look good. Not only did he embarrass her if he didn't like what she said, but he would often tell her exactly what to say and when. Most people don't like to witness marital conflicts, and I guess he never figured out that his belittling Margot in public made him look like the dumbass, not her.

"His verbiage was just as hurtful as any physical abuse. Margot told me it felt like he was always waiting for a buzz word to open the door and give him the opportunity to berate her and start a rift. He's your quintessential *showboat!* He puts on a good front, but Mr. Hyde is always lurking in

REFLECTION OF A KILLER — JUDITH BLEVINS & CARROLL MULTZ

the wings ready to pounce."

I listened intently without interrupting as Paige continued, "I seriously doubt that he ever loved her. Although Margot wanted a family, children were out of the question. Leonard's reasoning was, besides taking the chance that a pregnancy would ruin her figure, he didn't want brats running around his house, destroying it. Margot was what is typically known as a trophy wife. And to answer your unspoken question, Margot was afraid to leave him. Knowing what I know about him, and his determination to achieve his ultimate goal, I often wondered how he arranged the freak accident that resulted in the death of the incumbent the first time he ran for mayor. With him, the end always justified the means."

After a brief pause, Paige continued. "Becoming mayor and being in the public eye in a city as large as Denver, could be considered a substantial step toward the White House. After all, his publicity did get him into the Senate. Go figure!"

This one has a serious axe to grind, and if what she says is true, who can blame her? After pausing to assimilate the information Paige just revealed, I asked, "Did Leonard know about the blackmail?"

"Yes. He's the one who conjured up the story Margot told you about hitting a dog."

Sounds like a politician. "I assume the blackmail stopped once Leonard was elected?"

"I would suppose so. However, as I said, I wouldn't be surprised if Leonard staged the extortion to feather his own nest. He was always finding a way to invade funds coming from our side of the family. God only knows what he's stolen or sequestered away from his unsuspecting wife. Everything has always been about him!"

Suddenly, Paige began to weep. I felt like a brut when other customers in the coffee house looked in our direction. When I started to speak, she waved her hand in the air indicating she needed a minute to calm herself. I sat in silence and watched as she attempted to regain her composure.

When the moment was right, Paige stammered, "I was on the phone with Margot the night she was shot."

I had just barely recovered from the shock of finding out Leonard was responsible for the hit and run when Paige hit me with another shocker. Stunned, I blurted, "You were on the phone with her when she was shot!" Now it was my turn to take a moment to regain my composure.

"Yes. Her self-confidence was so low, she was reluctant to make decisions on her own, even regarding something as simple as a pair of sunglasses. The night she was shot, she called wanting my opinion regarding a pair of sunglasses she just purchased. She was streaming me videos of her posing in them.

"At Leonard's bidding, Margot was in the process of building a wardrobe suitable for her role as a senator's wife and she constantly wanted my reassurance she made the right choices. She didn't want to embarrass him. Like I said, her confidence was shattered, and she was even hesitant to make the simplest decisions on her own."

Still reeling from Paige's revelation, I finally got it together enough to ask, "Do the authorities know what you just told me?"

Paige shook her head. "No. At first, I didn't realize what had happened. I heard a loud bang, probably the shot, and then the phone went dead. I rationalized it could've been a car backfiring or someone slamming a door. I tried calling her back, without success. Since she didn't call me back, I assumed Leonard had come home and she couldn't talk freely so she just didn't answer my call."

Paige once again became emotional and putting a fist to her mouth, she bit down on her forefinger, apparently trying to stifle her sobs. I hesitated momentarily before asking the next question. "When did you find out about the…the death?"

"Leonard called later that night after the police left. He feigned shock and heartbreak over Margot's death," Paige managed to say. "It was an Academy Award performance."

I said, "After talking to you, I think you should go to the—"

Paige cut me off before I could finish the sentence. "I know who shot her!" she stammered.

"You do!" I exclaimed, unable to control my surprise.

"Yes, I'm sure I do. You see, that evening she was streaming me poses of her in her new sunglasses just before the shot was fired. When her phone went dead, I didn't bother looking for any more messages from her and didn't find the last video she sent until the following day. I was stunned when I viewed it. The video revealed an image which was reflected in her sunglasses of someone approaching her. I instantly recognized the image as Leonard. He walked with a distinct swagger, and I recognized his gait even though just a few steps were captured on the transmission before the phone went dead."

"And…and you're positive that it was Leonard?"

"Yes, one hundred percent positive! The video is grainy and if you didn't know him, you wouldn't be able to put two-and-two together. However, I know him and I'm positive it was Leonard."

"May I see it?" I asked.

By way of answering, Paige began scrolling through her iPhone apparently searching for the definitive evidence.

When she handed me her phone, I could barely see the image she was talking about. If I didn't know what I was looking for, I would have missed it completely. During his campaign, Leonard Lexington had plastered the countryside with placards of himself. Despite having seen his picture dozens of times, I couldn't swear the image revealed on Margot's sunglasses was his.

"What do you think?" Paige asked as I squinted at her cellphone.

"I donno," I responded. "It could be him. Can you expand it?"

Taking the phone from me, Paige went through the process of expanding the video and then handed the phone back to me. "Is that better?" she asked.

Since I was not personally acquainted with Leonard, I was not able to make a positive connection. I furrowed my brow as I strained to see what Paige was seeing. After a moment, she asked, "What do you think?"

"I'm still not convinced it's him," I replied. "The police should have Margot's cellphone in evidence, and they've most likely examined it."

"I thought of that as well and went to the police department as soon as I arrived in Denver. I was allowed to review the items taken into evidence since I'm her closest family member, that is, other than Leonard. Her cellphone was not among the items seized. I'm guessing Leonard must've destroyed it."

"If that's the case, you should turn this over to the detectives investigating Margot's death right away. They have technology lightyears beyond my comprehension. They would be able to enhance the image—"

"No! Can't do that! Don't you get it? Leonard was aware of Margot's and my close relationship. He probably reviewed the messages on her phone before he got rid of it. He must now know she told me about the accident and that he was the driver. Leonard has already killed once. Now that he's a member of the United States Senate, accusing him of Margot's murder would be signing my own death warrant. I'm sure he would have someone kill me and destroy the evidence just as he did in Margot's case. And whoever he asked would probably gladly do it to gain favor with a United States senator."

Paige paused before continuing, "It appears that our elected officials are immune from prosecution and are not required to adhere to the law like those they govern so they set out to feather their own nests before leaving office. Haven't you noticed, there's no integrity in government anymore?"

Anymore? When was there ever? Paige's concern was real and if Leonard killed once, what would stop him from doing so again. All is fair in love, war, and politics. Like any hardened criminal, they rationalize away all culpability. It's always someone else's fault!

Chapter Three

There Is No Free Lunch

"Hey, Cooper!" Detective Thornton bellowed into the receiver as soon as I picked up the phone. "Wheeler told us you did some work for Margot Lexington. You know something we should know?"

Perturbed at Thornton's attitude, I shot back, "Well, good morning to you, too."

"Okay, point made now cut the crap. We've got a lot of pressure on us to solve this one because of the husband's position. Feds think the senator's life could also be in jeopardy, so if you know something, you better tell us," Thornton snapped back.

"Or else...?" I teased.

"You're insufferable, you miserable piece of dog meat! What do you want in return?" Thornton asked.

"How 'bout some respect...and lunch!"

"You get both...as well as an apology. When and where do you want to meet?" Thornton asked.

I thought the *apology* was pretty weak, and still stinging from Thornton's attitude and the name calling, I wasn't in a generous mood. I'm like that—cut me once, I cut you ten times, so I picked a very expensive venue for lunch. "*The Lancaster*— fifteen minutes," I said.

"And here I thought you'd be a cheap date," Thornton sneered. "Meet you there, I'm on my way…and it better be worth it!"

• • •

Seated on the terrace overlooking the lake, we watched swans float effortlessly about on the surface for a few minutes.

"This is absolutely one of my favorite places," I mused just to slip in a zinger.

Thornton appeared to be anxious. Clearing his throat, he looked at his watch, and remarked, "This stroll through utopia is quite enchanting, but remember I'm on the city's payroll so let's cut to the chase."

Before I could respond, our waiter appeared. Thornton pointed to my menu and cocked his head to the side indicating for me to proceed.

"Okay. Think I'll have the house cheeseburger," I said to the waiter handing him my menu.

"Sounds wonderful. Think I'll have a glass of water," Thornton replied.

"Ah, come on," I joshed. "Live a little. You can't take it with you."

"Okay, I'll have a wedge of lemon with the water." He then said, as he also handed his menu to the waiter, "Just kidding, make that two cheeseburgers." After the waiter retreated, Thornton groaned, "Wife finds out about this lunch, I may be leaving earth sooner than expected…"

"I think you'll agree that what I'm about to reveal is worth this measly lunch," I said. As we consumed fifteen-dollar cheeseburgers, I filled Thornton in on my conversation with Paige. About midway through my narration, Thornton set his burger aside and stared at me.

"Hold on, partner. You're telling me the senator was driving that rainy night several months ago when the teen was hit and killed."

"That's correct! According to Paige, Margot's sister, Leonard was driving. Margot wasn't even with him. She never left the house the whole evening. Apparently, someone saw the accident and took down the license number. The car was registered to Margot Lexington, and she began receiving blackmail demands offering silence for cash."

"My God, man!" Thornton exclaimed. "Arresting and prosecuting a United States senator for a hit and run resulting in death and leaving the scene…" He then covered his face with his hands and moaned, "If that can be proven, we will've opened a nasty can of worms."

"Right you are but hold on. That's just the tip of the iceberg, my friend," I said.

"Oh, no! there's more?" Thornton whimpered removing his hands from his face.

"Your *nasty can of worms* is about to turn into a nastier pit of vipers. When you hear the rest, you may need medical attention."

I then told Thornton of Paige's accusation that the senator murdered his wife, and that she was an eyewitness, so to speak. When I explained to him that she had a video of the shooting on her iPhone, Thornton blanched. As the color drained from his face, I remarked, "Hey, partner, I was just kidding when I said you may need medical attention! Don't die on me now!"

Apparently, trying to assimilate the information just revealed, Thornton mumbled, "I can't believe our newly elected senator is capable of cold-blooded murder." He then sat up straighter and exclaimed, "That rotten SOB! I even campaigned for that bum!"

"I, too, found it hard to believe. When Paige revealed to me the contempt she had for Leonard and the way he treated her sister, my first thought was that Paige was seeking revenge for the way Margot was abused by her husband."

After a brief pause, I continued, "When I first

saw the video, I couldn't be sure it was Lexington. However, Paige was sure it was him, and she's more familiar with him than I am. I only knew him from television campaign ads, and the billboards and placards scattered across the state. She was so adamant, I'm compelled to believe her!" I remarked as I polished off my burger. Folding my napkin, I placed it on the table and asked, "So, where do we go from here?"

It was obvious from the sour expression on Thornton's face that he finally grasped the gravity of the situation. Tossing his napkin onto his plate, he snorted, "For cryin' out loud, Cooper! Why the hell didn't her sister come to us in the first place?"

I shrugged. "Age-old reason, I suppose. Fear that Lexington would kill her, too, if he found out about the video. She's terrified! After all, Paige basically witnessed him murdering his wife so why wouldn't he kill Paige to silence her as he did Margot?"

Thornton nodded. "Is Paige still in town?" he asked.

"Donno. When we last spoke, since she opted not to expose the video, she was eager to get back to Savannah. However, don't think we've heard the last of her. I get the impression she was totally devoted to Margot in life and now in death is committed to seeing that Leonard gets his just deserts."

"Man! Do you know what this means if it checks out?" Thornton barked. Then he snapped, "Do you have a number for her?"

I scrolled through my phone and finally came up with Paige's cell number. A few moments after placing the call, Thornton disconnected and glared at me. "You sure that's the right number?" he asked. I checked again and repeated it to him. He dialed it again. After a short wait, Thornton disconnected, "She doesn't answer. And I happen to know everyone carries their phone with them wherever they go. It's like the cellphone is an extension of the person. She apparently doesn't want to talk to anyone with a Denver area code. Looks like you've been bamboozled by another pretty face!"

When we parted in the parking lot, Thornton stated he was going to do some further investigation on both the hit and run and Margot's murder. I suggested that he also check the senator's bank accounts to see if maybe, just maybe, he was also the extortionist. Thornton just rolled his eyes and shook his head. Why hadn't he thought of that?

• • •

Upon his arrival back at the station, Thornton ran into Finn Doyle in the corridor and motioned him into his office.

"What's up?" Doyle asked as he closed the door behind him.

"Had lunch with Cooper," Thornton replied.

"Yeah! How'd you get so lucky?" Doyle teased.

"I called him, lunch was the *quid pro quo*. From the way Cooper was acting, I had a hunch he knew something about the Lexington murder he wasn't sharing with us. Remember, Wheeler told us that Cooper said he knew the victim."

"Yeah, and how is it Cooper's rubbing elbows with the rich and famous? Didn't think he traveled in the same social circles as the celebs," Doyle smirked.

"Wheeler said Cooper told him the vic wanted to hire him to investigate a matter for her and that's how he met her."

"That right? Wheeler say what kind of *matter*?" Doyle asked.

"No. However, it cost me a lunch, a very expensive lunch, but I found out, at least, according to Cooper, the vic's sister, Paige Fontaine, witnessed the murder, that is, so to speak," Thornton replied, giving Doyle that all-knowing look.

"What!" Doyle blurted. "And just how do you witness a murder *so to speak*?"

"Via modern technology, my friend," Thornton said. "Margot was in the process of streaming

Paige selfies of her posing in her new sunglasses. Paige claims, during the filming, the reflection in the glasses caught the image of the killer walking up to Margot and shooting her."

"Well, I'll be damned," Doyle uttered under his breath. "And all that was reflected in a pair of sunglasses?"

"That's what the sister claims," Thornton replied.

"Did she recognize the killer?"

"Yes, she claims it was our new senator, Leonard Lexington, the vic's husband," Thornton replied.

"Jesus, Joseph, and Mary!" After a pause, Doyle barked, "And it took this long for you to fill me in on that juicy bit of information. I'm hurt!"

"Well…I had to lay the groundwork and not just blurt it out," Thornton responded.

"Yeah, sure!" Doyle said then added, "Did Cooper confirm it was Lexington?"

"No. He said Paige showed him the video and he saw the image, but it was pretty vague. Said he couldn't tell who it was. I tried to call Paige," Thornton said, "but she doesn't answer. My guess is, since she didn't opt to bring the police on board in the first place, she's probably avoiding calls from this area code. Having witnessed the murder of her sister and then fearing for her own life is a pretty powerful reason not to come forward."

"Probably. What's our next move?" Doyle asked Thornton.

"Hang on to your hat, that's not all. Maybe you should take a seat."

"That bad, huh?" Doyle mumbled as he sat down.

"Yep, it's that bad. Paige related to Cooper that it was Leonard who hit and killed the teenager that rainy night several months ago."

"Come on! You can't be serious. This some kind of April Fool's joke?" Doyle asked.

"It's not April and it's not a joke. Margot told her sister she was being blackmailed by some unknown who happened to get her license number. She claimed Leonard had borrowed her car the night of the accident. Margot said Leonard threatened her if she didn't take the blame if it came to that."

Sliding back into his chair, Doyle sighed and asked, "You still have that bourbon in your desk drawer? I could use a stiff belt right about now."

"Me, too. Unfortunately, I gave it up last time I ran out."

• • •

After the meeting with Thornton, Doyle retreated to his office, closed his door, and dialed

Leonard Lexington's private telephone number.

"What is it?" Lexington answered in a gruff voice. His private cellphone was reserved for emergencies and then only by a select few.

"Paige, your sister-in-law, has been getting cozy with Cooper," Doyle began. "Apparently, she has a video on her phone of you offing Margot."

"What! How can that be?" Lexington gasped.

"Don't know the technology but it appears as you approached Margot, your image was captured in her sunglasses as she was streaming live poses to Paige. Cooper passed that info along to Thornton over lunch and Thornton just advised me of it. Paige also told Cooper you were driving Margot's car when the kid was killed in a hit and run."

"Son-of-a-bitch!" Lexington exclaimed followed by a long period of silence. He then asked, "What's the current situation?"

"Since Margot's dead, it's Paige's word against yours. But apparently you now have an even bigger problem to deal with. Thornton tried to call Paige on her cellphone, but she didn't answer."

"She probably left the country," Lexington remarked followed by another long silence. "We have to get that video! You have Kenny's number, and since we have no choice, you know what to do!! Getting rid of Paige will solve both problems. Keep me posted. I'm relocating to D.C. at the end of the week, but I'll always be available at this number."

"Roger that," Doyle said and hung up the phone. *Why didn't the dumb ass have Kenny do the job in the first place and avoid all this turmoil?*

Chapter Four

City of Lights

I don't like being disrespected, especially by cops who treat PIs like second-rate citizens. I took exception to Thornton's remark that I'd been bamboozled *by another pretty face*, and being very competitive, I decided to take it upon myself to find Paige—if for no other reason than to prove I could.

During our brief association, I remembered Paige saying that because of distance and health issues, their relatives living in Versailles would be unable to attend Margot's funeral. Since I had no idea where Versailles was, I did some research and found that it was only 15 miles from Paris. That sounded to me like a good place to start my search for Paige, so I booked a flight to Paris.

My research also revealed that the population of Versailles was only 85,700. If the Fontaines were an old, established family in that area I figured that someone should know something about them. I studied the map of Versailles and had an idea of the infrastructure and the major attractions of the city. The architecture was undeniably amazing. I'm intrigued by history, and as I perused the Internet, I marveled at the photographs of Marie Antoinette's Estate, the Palace of Versailles, the Gardens of the Palace of Versailles, and the Hall of Mirrors—all depicted on the Internet and advertised as the most-visited places.

I felt more comfortable at having done my homework on Versailles, so during the twelve-hour flight from Denver to Paris, I boned up on Paris—thanks to the brochures positioned in the seat pocket in front of me. I was surprised to learn that originally Paris' nickname, City of Lights, didn't necessarily refer to electric illumination. Apparently, in the late 18th, early 19th centuries, Paris was known as the center of education and reputedly the melting pot or think tank for intellectuals throughout Europe. The city was attributed to being an inspiration to poets, philosophers, engineers, and scientists from across the continent. Thus, I suspect it was considered a city of *enlightenment* and thus *City of Lights.* Who knows? Anyway, that's my take!

It was dark when my plane approached Charles de Gaulle airport preparing to land, and from the air, it was obvious that Paris was indeed a city of lights, literally. The most impressive sight from the air was the Eiffel Tower reaching 1,063 feet into the sky. The Tower was constructed of iron and steel, which elements were considered a great industrial advancement at the time of its erection. The company, founded and operated under the direction of engineer Gustave Eiffel, designed and built the Eiffel Tower and it was designated to be one of the main attractions at the Paris World's Fair in 1889. The Eiffel Tower is synonymous with Paris and is still one of Paris' main attractions along with the Louvre Museum and Notre Dame Cathedral. Surprisingly, the Eiffel Tower is not one of the seven wonders of the world.

Staring out of my window, I couldn't help smiling as I remembered that, in the spirit of competition, the American response to the Eiffel Tower was the Ferris Wheel. In 1893, it was America's turn to host the World's Fair. The Ferris Wheel, first of its kind, stood 264 feet high and was introduced at the Chicago World's Fair in 1893, four years after the Paris World's Fair beguiled the world with its Eiffel Tower. The Farris Wheel was and still is a testimony to American ingenuity. Much like the Eiffel Tower, the Farris Wheel was an unprecedented success and is still being enjoyed by millions of visitors and carnival-goers throughout the world.

• • •

Before leaving for Paris, I booked a room at the *Beaumont Hotel* in the Versailles' downtown area and when we deplaned, as soon as I retrieved my duffel bag from the luggage carousel, I grabbed the hotel shuttle. Several other travelers were shuttling to the *Beaumont* along with me, and the driver, whom I estimated to be in his mid-twenties, was identified by his nametag as Vincent Dubois. He doubled as tour guide and pointed out places of interest we may want to visit as we made the 15-mile trek through Paris on our way to the *Beaumont*.

"You seem to know your way around," I said upon our arrival at the hotel.

"Thank you, sir," Dubois replied. "I've lived in Versailles all my life."

Removing my duffel from the shuttle luggage compartment, I said, "I'm in need of someone with the history and knowledge of the area. Would you be available for hire when you're not driving the shuttle?"

"Yes, sir," Dubois said with exuberance. "My uncle runs the shuttle. He encourages his drivers to interact with our visitors and claims they will remember our friendliness and want to return. I'm often hired as an interrupter, so uncle allows me as much time off as needed."

My lucky day! "Okay! Does nine o'clock tomorrow work for you?" I asked.

"Yes, sir," Dubois responded, "I'll meet you

right here in front of the hotel."

• • •

At precisely 9:00 a.m., as I exited the *Beaumont*, I saw Dubois standing by an old pickup parked under the portico. "Bonjour," he greeted as he opened the passenger door.

"Hello and thank you. By the way, what do people call you?" I asked as I climbed into the truck.

Running around the front of the truck to the driver's side, and climbing in, he said, "Friends call me Vinny." Then flashing me a toothy grin, he patted the truck's dashboard and said, "This here's Coco."

"Vinny it is! Call me Jack." *Wonder how flattered Coco would be if she knew she had a beat-up pickup named after her.*

"Where do you want to go?" Vinny asked as he engaged the ignition. To my surprise, the engine purred like a kitten.

"I'm looking for someone. Perhaps you know the family. Their last name is Fontaine."

"Yes, sir! The Fontaines have been around these parts for many years," Vinny said. "The one's I know have a vineyard just outside of Versailles." After a pause, he asked, "Is that where you want me to take you?"

"Yes," I responded, "but for now just drive past. I…I want to surprise them."

Vinny put the truck in gear, and we sped at lightning speed from the hotel driveway. This was a far cry from the ultra-safe driving he displayed last night. I was surprised Coco had so much life in her. "Whoa, partner. We're in no hurry…" I cautioned.

"Oh, sorry, sir," Vinny said in an apologetic tone. "Uncle insists his drivers drive the shuttles in a fashion so as not to frighten the passengers. Guess I get carried away when I'm driving Coco."

"I understand," I said. "However, she certainly doesn't look like a racer. You have her souped up?"

"Souped up?" Vinny asked.

"You know, have the engine revved up," I explained.

"Oh, non! Did it myself. Working on engines is a hobby of mine. I keep both of Uncle Leon's shuttles in good running condition and do a little mechanic work on the side. Wouldn't do to have hotel guests stranded on the road somewhere between Paris and Versailles."

I was impressed with Vinny's mastery of the English language and his upbeat attitude. "Where'd you learn to speak English?" I asked.

"School. It's not a required subject, but it's a good skill to have especially with so many tourists visiting Paris from English-speaking countries. As you just found out, I don't know all the lingo."

I nodded. *Smart kid, and especially since English is considered a universal language.*

• • •

The Tuscan-style Fontaine villa, complete with a large swimming pool and manicured gardens, was situated on the top of a hill overlooking a very impressive vineyard. Swarms of pickers were busily working their way through the narrow rows between the vines gathering the grapes. Others collected them in horse-driven carts which were positioned at the end of the rows and transported them to what appeared to be the winery.

"Do you know the process for making wine?" Vinny asked, his eyes glued on the vineyard.
"Sure, wash your feet and stomp the hell outta the grapes," I jokingly replied.

"Good guess, but washing the feet is optional," Vinny smiled. "Where to now, boss?"

If Paige was there, I didn't want her to see me, anyway not just yet. If she was afraid of Lexington and for good reason, I worried I'd spook her, and if she ran again, I'd lose her again.

"Is there somewhere we can park without being observed and watch the comings and goings in and out of the villa? I want to make sure the main one

I'm searching for is here before I…well, you know, surprise her."

"Sure. There's a dirt road that encircles the estate. You can clearly see the entrances to the villa from several spots."

Vinny turned the truck around and drove Coco down a cow path masquerading as a dirt road. We took up position in a spot where we could see all the activity in and out of the estate. The morning and afternoon dragged by without any sign of Paige. Vinny brought a bottle of water for each of us for which I was extremely grateful. It was getting hot, and sitting for hours on Coco's hard seat, especially after yesterday's 12-hour plane trip, my travel-weary body was starting to talk to me. And needless to say, the conversation was painful. My butt, back, and brain were all numb. I finally said, "I give up. Let's head back to the hotel."

Vinny quickly engaged the engine and started back down the dirt road. He, apparently, was of the same mind.

• • •

It was noon when we arrived back at the *Beaumont*. After letting me out in front of the hotel, Vinny asked, "Same time tomorrow?"

I nodded and headed for the hotel's entrance. As I stepped into the revolving glass doors, I looked up and saw Paige. She was just entering the revolving doors from the interior of the hotel. It was apparent she didn't see me, so I pounded on the glass as the doors started to revolve attempting to get her attention but to no avail. Suddenly, the revolving stopped, and I was trapped in my section of the doors by a portly woman as she crammed herself and her oversized handbag between one of the four partitions. From my cocoon I watched Paige exit the hotel and head straight for a taxi that was waiting under the portico. A moment later, the revolving door started turning and I was soon free. I rushed out and much to my surprise, I noticed Vinny still maneuvering out of the hotel's driveway. I wildly waved my arms in an attempt to get his attention and rushed toward the truck. He apparently saw me and stopped. I ran up to the truck, jerked open the passenger door, and jumped in.

Vinny looked at me with questioning eyes. "Follow that taxi!" I ordered.

"You bettcha, boss. Just like in the movies, eh?" Vinny grinned and stomped on the gas just as traffic cleared.

The wild 15-mile ride from Versailles to Paris led us back to the airport. Vinny parked in a reserved parking spot and hung a handicapped placard from the rearview mirror.

When I raised my brow, he explained, "Sometimes it's necessary to park close to the entrance when I'm transporting handicapped in the shuttle, especially to the airport. I keep a placard in the truck because...you never know!"

"Never mind!" I replied. "Too much information!"

We rushed into the concourse just in time to see Paige stepping up to the Egyptian Skies counter. It appeared she was in the process of purchasing a ticket.

Egyptian Skies? What the hell. Is she now headed for Egypt? I watched Paige hand something to the clerk stationed behind the counter, probably a credit card to pay for a ticket. Paige then turned and headed toward the exit. Since she didn't have any luggage with her, I assumed the ticket was for a later date.

"Vinny, you follow her. Don't let her out of your sight. I'll take a taxi back to the hotel and meet you there later."

"Okay, boss, but you get me a ticket, too. I speak fluent Arabic, and you'll need me."

Is there anything this kid doesn't do? I mused as I approached the ticket counter.

"May I help you?" an attractive attendant dressed in a smart navy-blue *Egyptian Skies* uniform asked.

"Yes," I replied looking at the computerized arrival and departure flight schedules posted on the monitor on the wall behind her. I knew she couldn't tell me what flight Paige purchased a ticket for, so I asked, "What time is your next flight out?"

"To what destination?" she politely asked but her expression conveyed a different message— something like *Am I a mind reader?*

"Ah, doesn't matter. I just want the next flight out," I stammered.

I got the *look* again before she glanced at a clipboard, saying, "Next departure is not until tomorrow morning. It's our flight to Cairo and leaves at eight."

I took a deep breath and rolled the dice, hoping they didn't come up snake eyes. "Okay, I want two tickets on that flight," I said and reached in my rear pocket for my wallet.

"Do you want to check any luggage at this time?" the attendant asked as she processed the tickets.

"Ah, no, we'll bring our bags with us tomorrow. Thank you, anyway."

I'm sure I must have looked and acted suspicious but luckily the clerk didn't attempt to alert security— at least not in my presence. Being incarcerated in an

Egyptian jail trying to explain my peculiar actions didn't sound like a very good idea.

Having procured the tickets, I exited the airport and hailed a cab. *"Beaumont Hotel,"* I directed. As the driver blended into oncoming traffic, I turned and looked out the rear window. The fellow standing at the curb following my cab with hooded eyes looked mighty familiar. A sudden chill crept down my spine when I recalled seeing him accompanying Lexington during his campaign. *Is he following me?*

Chapter Five

Cairo

The next morning, I was disappointed when I didn't see Paige in the *Egyptian Skies* waiting area as we waited for our flight to be announced. I consoled myself thinking she could be running late or in the lady's room, or worst-case scenario, just not taking this flight. *What the hell! I've always been intrigued by, but never been to Egypt, so why not enjoy the excursion. Never mind the way my credit card is rapidly closing the gap between my balance and my limit.*

When we were called to board our flight and still no Paige, I decided to make the best of the situation. I still held out hope she'd show up and if not, perhaps when we returned to Paris, I'd catch up with her.

• • •

The flight time between Paris and Cairo was four hours and thirty minutes. Being in a foreign country intrigued me and I stayed alert the whole flight. Our fellow travelers were a mixture of cultures, and I was thankful Vinny talked me into bringing him along. His interpretation skills saved me a lot of embarrassment. Besides, he was good company and my security blanket.

Nearing the end of our flight, I asked Vinny, "Have you ever visited the pyramids?"

"Only in history books and travel magazines," he replied. "Do you plan on taking one of the tours to the pyramids while you're in Cairo?"

"Hadn't thought about it," I replied. "Being in Cairo wasn't planned. However, I'd like to go on one of the tours if circumstances and time allow."

"A once-in-a-lifetime opportunity," Vinny replied. "Cairo is only eight miles from the Giza Plateau where three of the most famous pyramids are located. However, I understand there are over seventy pyramids still standing in different locations up and down the Nile River Valley."

The Sahara Desert passed beneath our plane as we prepared for landing, and I had my face plastered against the small window as we spoke. Being more accustomed to the majesty of the Colorado Rockies, I was intrigued by the desert and when the three Giza pyramids came into view, they took my breath away.

"And I thought the Eiffel Tower was impressive," I muttered. Mesmerized by the view and dumbfounded at the thought of how much labor must've been involved in the erection of the giants, I whispered, "How'd they do that over four thousand years ago?"

Vinny leaned forward and stared past me out the window. Profoundly he uttered in a soft tone, "The mystery of how they were erected by the ancients keeps luring the *hungry* back to Giza seeking answers. That mystery keeps pumping life's blood into the region. Archaeologists, historians, scholars, the curious, the thrill-seekers, and the just plain mystified come and go at an alarming rate."

Without taking my eyes from the view passing below us, I asked, "Which category do you fall into?"

I waited, and when Vinny didn't answer, I turned from the window. That's when I saw one of the *Egyptian Skies* flight attendants standing in the aisle beside our seat. She looked familiar even though she wore a hijab wrapped around her head.

"Hmm, I think I'm one of the just plain mystified," the flight attendant said, apparently having overheard our conversation. "However, I don't discount the theory that the ancients could've had help from the elusive aliens we're always hearing about. And if you pause to think about that mind-boggling concept, you become even more mystified."

Then it hit me. *Paige!* "What...what are you doing here?" I stammered.

Pointing to the name tag pinned to her uniform jacket, she said, "I work here." Gathering our lunch remains into a plastic trash bag, Paige continued, "Airline employees layover in Cairo at the *Pharoah*. I'll meet you there in the lounge at three."

Having thought I'd lost her again, It took me a few minutes to gather my wits at Paige's uncanny appearance. And a flight attendant none-the-less!

• • •

Vinny and I retrieved our bags from the luggage carousel and exited the airport. Once outside, we engaged a taxi that was parked at the curb waiting for a fare from arrivals. Vinny conversed with the cabbie in Arabic and learned, since this was the off-season, there were accommodations available citywide. We were able to secure two side-by-side rooms at the *Pharoah* where Paige would be staying.

As we rode the elevator up to our rooms, Vinny said, "Boss, I think you should meet with the lady alone. She may be intimidated by my presence, so I'll just take a walk around the city and get a feel for things."

I looked at him in amazement. Not only did he speak several languages fluently, he was also intuitive. "That's a great idea! Let's meet back here around six for dinner," I suggested.

"Okay, but for your information, dinner is

usually served between nine and ten in this part of the world," Vinny replied.

"What! I'll be dead by then," I moaned.

"In that case, you may want to grab a snack from one of the street stalls strewn up and down the avenues," Vinny remarked with a wide grin.

"Ugh! No thanks," I groaned. "I'd rather die of starvation than eat the fly-infested bill-o-fare offered by the street venders."

Pointing to my girth, Vinny commented: "I think you could live off the fat of the land—for a few hours anyway."

I prided myself on staying fit and trim and was insulted by the inference that I was fat and out of shape. I jerked my thumb in the direction of my door and ordered, "Out with you. Dinner or no dinner, I'll meet you back here around six."

• • •

The dimly lit lounge cooled by overhead oscillating ceiling fans and soft music, the local variety, muted the conversations swirling around me. As I sat at the bar waiting for Paige, I ordered one of the native brews. Examining myself in the mirror behind the bar, I sucked in my gut and sat a little straighter. *Damn smart-ass kid. Now I'm self-conscious.* However, I didn't have time to dwell on the subject as Paige's reflection in the mirror caught my attention. I turned, and when she saw me, she waved and pointed to one of the empty tables. I nodded and taking my glass, followed her to a table for two. When the bartender approached, she ordered iced tea.

Paige had with her a small flight bag which she secured at her feet. Apparently, noticing the perplexed expression on my face, she remarked, "I'll check into the hotel later. The airline has a contract with the *Pharoah* to provide rooms for employees who layover. It's very convenient. Also, my employer frowns on its employees drinking alcohol in public places since Egypt is mostly populated by Muslims. However, I carry several travel-size bottles with me and usually have a nightcap in my hotel room."

"I see," I said. "Like the Boy Scouts, you come prepared."

She smiled but looked uncomfortable. I finally said, "You kinda left me holding the bag—"

She put up a restraining hand. "I know and I apologe. Please, let me explain before you chastise me!"

I sat back in my chair and folding my arms across my chest, I said, "Okay, go ahead, explain!"

Paige swirled the ice in her glass and took a sip of tea before beginning. "Margot and Leonard had a whirlwind courtship," she said. "When they first met, Leonard had just graduated from law school. He was good looking and enthusiastic. Margot was fresh and beautiful. They complimented each other, and to outsiders, looked like the perfect couple."

Paige paused and closed her eyes, apparently trying to remember details. I waited in silence. After a moment, she then continued, "After completing an internship, Leonard was hired on as an associate by a Denver law firm. His expertise was international law and after a few years, he was made a partner. With Leonard's salary increase, they bought an impressive mansion and appeared to be living the American dream." Paige looked down at her hands which were now folded in her lap, and whispered, "They seemed to be so happy together in the beginning, I don't know when all of that changed."

When the waiter came by, I switched to iced tea. After it arrived, I tipped my glass toward Paige, "You've converted me," I teased. She gave me a weak smile. "Please, go on," I urged.

"Leonard was spending a lot of time out of country, mostly in the middle east. He told Margot his travels were related to his expertise in international law. When Margot became patently lonely, I provided her with a copy of my work schedule and invited her to call me anytime I was off duty. She began calling almost every evening when I wasn't flying. Sure, with Leonard gone so much of the time, she would be lonely! Margot and I were pretty much in sync with each other, and from her conversation, I sensed something more serious was wrong.

"The day after the hit and run traffic accident, Margot called and broke down. She said, 'Paige, I'm in big trouble. There was a terrible accident last night. Leonard was driving under the influence and hit and killed a teen.'

"I remember asking Margot at the time if Leonard was arrested. She said, 'No. He left the scene and now wants me to take the blame in the event the accident is traced back to *us*.'"

Taking a deep breath, Paige paused momentarily. She then continued saying, "I was furious to think that Leonard would do that to Margot, or anyone else for that matter. When I started to speak, Margot cut me off. 'Wait! That's not all! I have reason to believe Leonard is involved in an illegal oil deal with the Sabenese.' When I started to ask for details as to why she thought that, she cut me off once again and rushed on. She told me, 'I discovered some correspondence as I was dusting the top of Leonard's desk and was able to piece together evidence that the Sabenese basically insured Leonard's senatorial election by pumping large amounts of money into his campaign. In essence, they bought him the Senate seat! I'm sure there's a *quid quo pro*. I don't know what he's expected to do in return, but it can't be in the best interest of our country. As you well know from your travels abroad, the Sabenese are not America's friends. They're users and abusers and not allies!'"

Paige looked at me and I sensed she was close to tears, so I remained silent to allow her time and space to her tell her story in her own time and in her own way. She finally continued, "If Leonard checked Margot's phone log, he'd be aware that she talked to me quite often and probably told me everything she knew. After Margot's funeral, it suddenly dawned on me that, in order to continue with his nefarious dealings, Leonard would also have to shut me up. If he'd kill his wife, what would stop him from killing me or anyone else who posed a threat. On several occasions during the time I was in Denver, I observed one of Leonard's bodyguards stalking and spying on me, especially after I met with you." She looked up at me and grimaced, "Didn't want to get either one of us killed, so that's why I ran."

I reached across the table and caressed her hand.

"Would this *bodyguard* have hooded eyes?" I asked.

"Yes, that's a good way to describe him! How'd you know?" Then after a brief pause, she added, "Oh, no! He's here in Cairo, isn't he?"

"I saw him outside the airport in Paris. I don't know if he's in Egypt, but I suspect so," I replied.

Paige said pensively, "During one of our conversations, Margot described a weird man with *a brow sporting a deep-set crease* who worked for Leonard. She said his name was Kenny and that he gave her the creeps."

I nodded and said, "I'm sure that's the same man who tailed me here. When I saw you leave *The Beaumont* in Versailles, I followed you to the airport in Paris and the hooded-eyed stalker must've watched me purchase tickets to Cairo."

Paige quickly looked over her shoulder, apparently expecting to see the stalker creeping up behind her. Looking back at me, she asked, "Tickets?"

"Yes. Vinny, the young man seated next to me on the plane accompanied me. He's my tour guide and interpreter." After a pause, I asked, "How long is your layover here in Cairo?"

"Three days. We fly back to Paris on Monday."

When I looked at my watch, I realized I hadn't set it to local time. "Do you know what time it is?"

I asked as I prepared to make the adjustment.

Looking at the pendant watch she wore around her neck, Paige replied, "Five forty-five, on the button."

After I set my watch and picked up the check, I said in a low voice, "I've got to get going but don't want to leave you alone especially since we figured Kenny is on the prowl. I'm meeting Vinny at six for dinner. Would you like to join us?"

Without hesitation, Paige answered in the same tone of voice, "I would, and thank you for your concern. I'm beginning to feel like a sitting duck." She then stood and picked up her flight bag and draped the strap over her shoulder, "I know a quaint little restaurant off the beaten path that starts serving dinner at six. It's popular with tourists from the European continent. Like the song says, *they get too hungry for dinner at eight...*"

"Eight? You're a lifesaver! I heard the protocol here is dinner at nine!"

• • •

I waited as Paige checked into the hotel. We then picked up Vinny and headed for the restaurant Paige recommended. *The Iteru* translates to *The River* in English, and it was within walking distance of the *Pharoah*. I was delighted to find that it was situated so close to the Nile. As we strolled along the river front, Vinny regaled us with some of the information he picked up during his excursion earlier in the afternoon.

Sounding like a college professor, Vinny began, "The Nile is the longest river in the world and is rightfully nicknamed the *Father of African Rivers.* It flows northward through Africa to eventually meet the Mediterranean Sea. During ancient times, it was central to the rise of wealth and control of the Egyptians and was the lifeblood of Egypt. That was, of course, long before oil was discovered," Vinny said and flashed us one of his patented toothy grins.

Vinny took center stage and over dinner he filled us in on his trek around the city. "I took one of the tour busses that doesn't stop anywhere. The driver points out the high spots to the passengers to be visited later if the tourists so desire. When we passed close to the Nile, we could see whitewater rafters and watched swimmers and kayakers exploit the river." Through a mouthful of broiled fish, Vinny added, "The water looked inviting but that's not for me! Although we didn't see any, I've heard the river is infested with crocodiles." Then looking down at his plate, he added, "I'd rather eat the fish than have them eat me!"

"Smart boy!" Paige commented and gave him a salute with her wine glass.

I nodded and joined Paige in the salute.

Vinny continued describing his afternoon adventure. "Other points of interest were the Egyptian Museum which houses antiquities including royal mummies and King Tut's cache of golden artifacts according to the bus driver slash tour guide. I was surprised to hear that there was a cache of gold after hearing the stories about the tomb robbers and how they pilfered the pyramids," Vinny added.

Our waiter appeared and cleared our dinner dishes, after which he produced a tray containing three small cups and a brass pot of coffee. When he poured the coffee, its consistency looked more like syrup that liquid. I remember thinking, *if I drink that, I'll be awake for months.*

Taking a sip of the brew, Vinny winced, and pushed his cup aside. "Think I'll pass," he murmured and continued with his rendition, "We passed the very impressive Cairo Tower, which is the tallest structure in Egypt at six hundred and fourteen feet. It's even taller, if you can believe it, than the Great Pyramid and from its top, you can see the city and all the pyramids at Giza."

"Sounds like you had quite the tour," I said. "Too bad we don't have time to explore the city in more depth."

"Right! It's truly fascinating," Vinny responded.

I glanced at Paige. "Have you toured the pyramids?" I asked.

"I'm ashamed to say I have not," she replied. "I've been doing the Paris slash Cairo turn for a couple of years now but haven't been to the pyramids yet." Then after a pause, Paige added, "However, they're at the top of my bucket list."

Vinny interrupted, "By the way," he said, "it's a small world. One of the passengers on the bus looked familiar. I could swear I'd seen him before—maybe in Paris."

Red flags immediately shot up. "What did he look like?" I anxiously asked.

"Hmm, pretty normal except for his eyes. That's what made me think I'd seen him before. The lids were very…unusual."

I glanced at Paige. All the color had drained from her face and her hands were shaking.

Can't get rid of a bad penny… or a curse! I reflected thinking of both the hooded-eyed stalker and King Tut.

Chapter Six

Cat and Mouse

Back at the hotel, we split up and retired to our respective rooms. Having Vinny confirm that Kenny or his identical twin was indeed in the vicinity, unnerved me. Sitting on the edge of my bed, I looked around my room and determined the venue was less than secure. The balcony doors were louver and looked as though a two-year-old could breach them. The lock on the entry door was ancient and appeared it could be opened with an old-fashion type skeleton key, or a penknife if one had the skill to do so. I was concerned for Vinny and myself, but even more so for Paige since she was the one who had the evidence that could seal Lexington's fate once and for all. It was obvious, any amateur could easily break in our suites—especially a seasoned killer like Kenny.

Rather than spending time fretting, I called Paige's room.

"Yes," she answered.

"It's Jack. Are you alright?"

"Not sure how to answer that," she replied, and I detected her voice quiver. "Physically I am.

Mentally and emotionally I'm a wreck."

"I know what you mean. I've been sitting here pondering our situation. After taking stock of the cracker box construction of our hotel rooms, I'm thinking the three of us should change hotels. We could share a two-bedroom suite. Vinny and I in one bedroom and you in the other. Safety in numbers! What do you think?"

"What do I think?" she said with exuberance in her voice. "I'm packing as we speak! By the way, do you have a firearm with you?"

"I do. I have a carry permit and was allowed to take *Old Faithful* aboard in my luggage when I embarked on this adventure," I said. "Do you have one?"

"No. But after this experience, I'm thinking about getting one when and if I live long enough to get back to Savannah."

"That's a great idea, and I personally guarantee you will get back to Savannah. In the meantime, we'll stick together. Vinny and I will meet you in the lobby as soon as we can get our stuff repacked," I said.

• • •

On the way to our rooms, Vinny had told me he was pretty beat and was going to turn in right away. So, before I rousted him, I made several phone calls finally securing a two-bedroom suite at *The Ra*. I then rang Vinny's room and rousted him. He said, in a sleepy voice, the only thing he unpacked was his toothbrush, so he was ready to go on a moment's notice. Vinny and I then met Paige in the *Pharaoh's* lobby, and after checking out, we took a taxi to The *Ra*.

Paige stared out of the cab's window as we traversed the streets of Cairo. It was obvious she was deep in thought no doubt pondering her situation and I was surprised when she finally spoke. Referring to ancient Egyptian mythology, she said, "*Ra* is the sun god, and my favorite Egyptian mythological god. His claim to fame was that he was *the* first pharaoh and ruled until he was too old to do so, or so the legend goes."

"Un-huh. And how old might that be," I asked.

"Good question," Paige replied. "Who knows?"

"That is a good question," Vinny replied. "And one I think I can answer."

I slumped back into the seat, *Of course, you can. I should've known,* I thought.

Vinny continued, "My field trip today was very informative. I learned that the ancients had a very high infant fatality rate, mostly due to infections. Plus, if the offspring survived infanthood, many children died before reaching the age of nineteen.

Those who lived didn't fare much better by today's standards. The life expectancy for women was thirty years and men thirty-four years." Vinny paused, before continuing, "It's estimated the Great Pyramid took twenty years to erect. If between thirty and thirty-four was the average life span and you consider the death rate among the tens of thousands, if not millions of slaves doing backbreaking work in the desert heat, it staggers the imagination to ponder the turnover. It's a wonder there were enough males left to propagate the race!"

Before anyone could speak, Vinny continued, "So Ms. Paige, I agree with your earlier assessment that aliens may have visited earth four or five thousand years ago. And if so," Vinny continued, "if they had the technology to move mountains and turn them into pyramids, so to speak, why wouldn't they also have had advanced medicines to help extend the Egyptian lifespan?"

I'm impressed. This kid's a deep thinker. I stared at Vinny and remarked, "That is indeed a provocative concept."

Vinny just frowned. *Was it my vocabulary?*

"Here ya are, folks," the cabbie announced as he pulled up under *The Ra's* portico.

When we entered *The Ra*, I scanned the lobby

halfway expecting to see the infamous Kenny lurking about. If he was, he was either well-hidden or well-disguised.

. . .

Our suite was on the seventh floor. It was decorated with ancient replicas of pottery and artwork that reflected life in Egypt centuries ago. The scenes depicted a tranquil life along the Nile. I couldn't help but reflect on Vinny's narration during our taxi ride of how hard life must really have been for the greater population. It appeared all life, other than royalty, revolved around pleasing the pharaohs and other Egyptian gods. They obviously had little time or energy for themselves.

Each of the two bedrooms had a sliding glass door that opened onto a shared balcony. I examined the locks on the outside door and the balcony doors. They all seemed to be sturdy—at least sturdier than those at the *Pharoah*.

Paige immediately went to her bedroom, but before she closed her door, she smiled at me, and squeezing my hand, said, "Thanks, Jack. I feel safer already."

Vinny didn't waste much time either. He headed directly into our shared bedroom suite, stretched out on his bed and was soon sound asleep. *Ah, to be young and carefree again!* I thought knowing my sleep would most likely be sporadic at best at least this night. After showering, I retrieved *Old Faithful* from my duffel and made sure it had six rounds in the chamber. I placed the weapon under my pillow and went to the balcony door. When I slid it open, although muted this high up, I could hear sounds of the city penetrating the night. The evening was clear and cool and when I stepped out, I saw Paige curled up on one of the chaise lounges on her side of the balcony.

"Nice evening," I said. "How long have you been out here?"

"Only a few minutes," she replied, gathering her robe closer around her. "I'm too nervous to sleep."

I walked to the edge and looked over the balcony railing. The street below was teaming with energy. People were bustling about, and cars were racing up and down the streets. I could even hear the venders seven stories below touting the virtues of their wares. I turned to Paige, "To be called *City of the Dead*, Cairo sure sounds alive to me."

"It's kinda like New York, you get used to the noise," Paige remarked. "Even the sound of blaring car horns."

"I can only hope," I said. "Vinny is sound asleep resting peacefully under the protection of Tutu."

Sounding surprised, Paige blurted, "*Tutu?* I didn't know you were into Egyptian mythology."

"Oh, I'm not really. I just pick up bits-and-pieces here-and-there to make me sound informed," I responded. "However, I like *Tutu*, the god who guards the sleeping—protecting them from danger. We could all use his special talents."

Paige smiled. "Umm, since I've been assigned to the Paris slash Cairo turn, I've become fascinated with ancient Egyptian history and mythology. Egyptian culture was extremely sophisticated for its time, but even primitive people worshiped some sort of deity and created icons to represent their gods. Millenniums before Christ was born, it appears that humans instinctively knew there was a power greater than themselves. There's evidence mankind recognized there was a supernatural power and erected places to worship their idols. For example, the stone heads on Easter Island and the Aztec and Inca pyramids in South America.

Pensive, Paige added, "Life must've been sacred from the beginning of time because, not only humans but other living creatures, were sacrificed on altars to appease the gods. However, humans must've been the supreme form of sacrifice. Even the Bible relates the story of Abraham being willing to sacrifice his only and most beloved son, Isaac, to God. Although God stopped him, the intent was still there."

Very profound. Between Paige and Vinny, I think I'm surrounded by deep thinkers, and I love the brain stimulation and challenge to think outside the square. Won't need a World Encyclopedia as long as I'm with them!

Gazing up at the starlit sky, Paige said reflectively, "I don't know if *they're* out there, but they certainly could be. Otherwise, how could the ancients have accomplished marvels even beyond our modern-day capabilities?"

"I know," I said, remembering how awestruck I was when I first saw the pyramids from the air as we were preparing to land in Cairo. I could spend hours pondering the creation of the pyramids and life itself, but we had bigger problems to cope with in our current situation, so I changed the subject. "Do you have your cellphone with you?"

"Yes. I always carry it, and especially now. It's my insurance policy," Paige said and glanced toward her bedroom probably to reassure herself her iPhone was safe, and that all was well. She then continued, "However, as an added precaution, I sent a copy of the video to my desktop in Savannah— just in case I lose the phone. FYI, if something happens to me, the video is filed on my desktop under the title *Ricochet"*

"Ricochet?" I quired.

"Yep! My sister didn't deserve to die, and especially not at the hands of that monster. My hope is that the video will boomerang, so to speak, and Leonard will spend the rest of his life in a prison cell—and even that would be too good for the sorry SOB."

Appreciating her depth of grief, I nodded and leaned against the wrought iron railing. When I did so, I felt a slight movement. "Whoa!" I said and immediately stepped away from the precarious railing. Peering down at the street below, I said, "This railing isn't very sturdy, someone could get hurt or even killed if it gave way. I'll report it to the manager first thing tomorrow morning. In the meantime, be very careful and stay as far away from the edge as possible."

"Roger that and you be sure to warn Vinny."

"Will do," I responded. There was a brief lull in the conversation, and I finally asked, "Have you changed your mind about going to the cops?"

Paige looked thoughtful for a moment, then answered, "Yes. I suspect somehow Leonard found out I have *the* evidence needed to prove he killed Margot and my life will no doubt be pure hell from now on. Since I'm obviously being stalked, the video apparently no longer is a best kept secret." After a brief pause, Paige added, "I can't go on living like this. I have a kink in my neck from looking over my shoulder all the time." She looked at me, and with a confused expression, queried, "By the way, how do you think Leonard found out I had an incriminating video?"

Her unbridled fear made me feel guilty, and she had the right to know, so I confessed. "After meeting with you following the funeral and carefully considering the events that took place," I began, "I came to the conclusion there must be a mole in the police department."

"Why would you think that?" she asked in a voice laced with anxiety.

"After you left Denver, I was confronted by Detective Russel Thornton. I previously let it slip to the medical examiner that I had done some work for Margot. The ME must've related that information to Thornton, and when Thornton confronted me, he said he thought I knew more than I was saying and asked me to help them out. Apparently, the department was being pressured to solve the murder. Their deduction was that Leonard most likely was the intended murder victim—not Margot. Since Leonard claims he wasn't home at the time of the murder, it's believed Margot just got in the way when the killer entered their home, and she had to be eliminated."

"Okay, go on," Paige urged impatiently.

Her gaze was accusatory, and I felt uncomfortable. *Now I know how my clients must feel when I interrogate them.* "Under the circumstances," I continued, "I told Thornton about you, and what appeared to be a video of Leonard shooting Margo as reflected in Margot's sunglasses and that you had the evidence on your iPhone."

"What! You did what? No wonder I'm being stalked. How could you?" Paige said and glared at me.

Already feeling like a Benedict Arnold, I was quick to jump to my defense. "I trusted Thornton and still do. My guess is he told someone else and that someone else is in Lexington's corner and maybe even on his payroll." I paused long enough to reflect on the consequences of revealing my suspicions to Paige. In her state of mind, no telling what she might do.

"And do you have any idea *who* that someone else might be!" she barked in a hostile tone of voice.

"Yes, I do!" I was quick to answer. Then in a calmer voice, said, "It's only logical Thornton would tell his partner, Finn Doyle. Never trusted that bastard Doyle, and my guess is he's the mole.

He's the type that would sell his mother for a dime."

Paige didn't respond immediately, and I watched her close her eyes and press her fingertips against her temples. "I'm frightened and confused—I don't know what to do next," she said. Then looking at me, she added, "And I apologize for my rudeness. I realize you were only doing what you thought was right to help bring Margot's murderer to justice."

"Thank you for that but it's me who should apologize to you! In retrospect, and knowing what I know now, I would have handled that meeting with Thornton much differently needless to say," I said. "Anyway, why don't we try to get some sleep. Tomorrow may be a long day for all of us."

Paige nodded and went back into her room. When she turned out her light, I headed for my room. Inside I glared at myself in the bathroom mirror and kicked myself around for having *betrayed* Paige's trust. Suddenly, I was both mentally and physically exhausted. I turned off the light and went to bed hoping to sleep through the night, despite the noise wafting up from the street below.

• • •

Kenny Clarkson had been standing watch and when the trio showed up in the *Pharoah's* lobby, he followed them to *The Ra*. From his vantage point he watched them check in. After they departed for the elevator, Kenny approached the desk clerk and procured their room number by slipping the clerk the equivalent of $50.00 in U.S. currency. For another $50.00 he was able to obtain a universal key card from a member of the cleaning staff.

Kenny was a patient killer and he now stood in the shadows waiting. A couple of hours into his wait, he checked his watch. It was 1:30 a.m. He knew most people, especially weary travelers, would be sound asleep in the wee hours and easy targets.

Although the contract was for the woman only, his employer had no way of knowing about the other two would-be witnesses. Kenny decided the two would also have to be eliminated—free of charge. The challenge was to locate their cellphones, and especially the woman's, before an alarm could be sounded.

Kenny took the elevator to the seventh floor of *The Ra*. He paused before his targets' door and listened. No sound came from inside and there was no one else around, so he skillfully inserted the universal key card into the slot and carefully opened the door to the suite. Stepping inside and carefully closing the door behind him, Kenny took a moment to orient himself. There was ample illumination filtering into the suite from the lights of a city which was still teeming with activity. Kenny was able to maneuver his way through the suite without making any noise or bumping into anything.

The door to one of the bedrooms was slightly ajar and the motion of a curtain swaying in the breeze caught Kenny's attention. When he looked further into the room, he noticed the bed was empty. It was obvious someone was on the balcony, so he crept to the balcony door and peered out. There he saw the woman who appeared to be sound asleep on a chaise lounge. Kenny recognized her as target number one, and she was within reach. He carefully slid the balcony door open far enough to squeeze through. When he did so, the door made a slight screeching sound. Kenny froze. He watched the woman stir slightly but she didn't appear to have awakened. Confident he had not been detected, he stepped out onto the balcony with a six-inch stiletto in his hand and at the ready. Kenny liked to kill with his knife. It was quiet, up close, and personal.

• • •

Since Margot's death, Paige's anxiety prevented her from falling into a deep slumber. She was restless and not completely asleep when she heard the balcony door slide open. The slight screech alerted her, and she came instantly awake. Now, paralyzed with fear, she lay perfectly still, even with her eyes closed she could sense someone moving about on the balcony. Moments, that seemed to her more like hours, passed and finally when she could pretend to be asleep no longer, she sprang into action. In one fell swoop, she tossed the blanket aside, and emitting a terrified scream as she sprang up from the lounge.

· · ·

Kenny was sure Paige was sound asleep. When she screamed, he was so startled, he jumped back colliding with the loose wrought iron railing. The sudden thrust of his weight against the railing caused it to break free from the balcony. Horrified, Paige watched Kenny, entangled in the railing, fall backward off the balcony onto the pavement seven stories below. Screams, screeching tires, and honking horns penetrated the night as Kenny splattered onto the street.

· · ·

I was instantly wide awake when I heard Paige's scream followed by the commotion on the balcony. Vinny, too, had aroused from his sleep and together we rushed out onto the balcony. Paige was kneeling on the tile floor with her hands covering her face. I gently took her hands in mine and helped her to her feet. She grabbed me around the waist and clung to me. Burying her face in my chest, she sobbed,

"He…he had a knife. I saw it when I jumped up. When I screamed, he fell backward onto the railing which gave way under his weight." After a pause, Paige stammered, "Jack, he…he tried to kill me!"

It was obvious she was in a state of shock. I took her by the shoulders and helped her back into her bedroom. Vinny had ventured to the edge of the balcony and was peering at the scene unfolding below. I motioned for him to follow us. I remembered Paige telling me she carried mini bottles of liquor with her on her trips. I rummaged through her purse and found a bottle of bourbon and poured it into a glass of ice. She struggled when I pressed it to her lips but after the first taste, she accepted the drink and took a gulp—and then another.

"Are you okay?" I asked.

"No! I'm a complete wreck!" Paige stammered. "I came within an inch of being killed and watched my would-be assassin fall seven stories to his death and you ask if I'm okay."

"What I meant was, are you physically hurt in any way," I explained.

"Oh, no, I don't think so," she whispered. She was still shaking so I coaxed her into taking yet another sip of bourbon. She then continued, "When I came back into my bedroom after our conversation, I was unable to fall asleep. Restless, I tossed and turned for over an hour and then decided to give it up and go back out onto the balcony. The slight breeze was cooling, and I curled up on the chaise lounge with a blanket and was dozing. Then all hell broke loose, figuratively and literally."

I took her in my arms and stroked her hair. "It's alright now. Just calm down."

Paige melted against me again and began to sob. "When is it ever going to end?" she murmured several times. I wondered the same thing.

REFLECTION OF A KILLER — JUDITH BLEVINS & CARROLL MULTZ

Chapter Seven

Pyramids Along the Nile

"That bumbling idiot!" Lexington shouted when Doyle told him about Kenny's *accident*. "I guess you realize the video is still out there and now Paige, after the attempt on her life, has more than enough reason to expose me as her sister's killer."

Doyle, seated cross legged in one of the leather chairs in Lexington's Denver office, was not intimidated by the senator's ranting. It was an everyday occurrence. "Easy, senator," Doyle said, "if you'd let Kenny take care of Margot in the first place—"

Lexington stood and leaned across his desk just inches from Doyle's face. "How dare you preach to me! Do you know who you're talking to?" Lexington snorted. "This is all *your* fault," he snarled jabbing his forefinger into Doyle's chest. "Remember, Kenny taking care of Paige was *your* suggestion!"

"Hold on, partner!" Doyle snapped, and slapped Lexington's hand away from his chest. Although Doyle's voice was calm, it was laced with venom and Lexington apparently knew he'd gone too far so he sat back down. "If *you* remember, *senator*, I suggested Kenny after *you* botched it up with Margot. If you think you're going to pin one damn thing on me, you've got another think coming."

Moments passed as the men glared at each other, neither one flinching or backing down. Finally, it appeared all the fight had gone out of Lexington, and he slumped back into his leather office chair. "Sorry, Finn. I didn't mean anything. I'm just anxious and overwrought. And to make matters worse, this morning, I got a call from Ammon, Sahib Abakali's secretary. It appears the Sabenese are ready to go now that I'm in the Senate and appointed to the Foreign Relations Committee as well as the Subcommittee on Trade and in a position to propose the deal on the oil glut. I'm in a tight spot. Since they basically ensured my election by pumping millions into my campaign, I'm indebted to them big time, and they expect a decent return on their investment."

Doyle appeared to be unmoved by the senator's plight. After all, who could blame him after having been shown no respect and treated like a lacky by the senator. Obviously, feeling less than generous, Doyle remarked, "You knew *that* when you accepted their money. So don't go complaining to me about the *quid pro quo!* Have you presented the Saudi's proposal to the Senate's Subcommittee on Trade and the Foreign Relations Committee?"

"Of course not!" Lexington bellowed. "How could I take the chance. With Paige still at large and in possession of evidence that could incriminate me as a murderer, I'd be a fool to go ahead with the Sabanese proposal. I don't want to think of what the consequences would be if I involved them in an international incident involving the murder of an American citizen."

Looking relaxed as he studied his nails in a blatant display of disrespect, Doyle asked, "So, where do we go from here?"

Lexington, apparently having had enough of Doyle's arrogance, stood and slammed his fist against his desktop, shouting as he then pointed a threatening finger at Doyle. "Not we! You! You… you do whatever it takes to find Paige and silence her—permanently! And make damn sure you retrieve the cellphone and any other incriminating evidence."

• • •

Now it was Doyle who apparently realized he'd gone too far. He had no respect for Lexington as a man, but he knew Lexington had resources to deal with the likes of him, a mere bought assassin. Returning to the police department, Doyle went to his supervisor's office and requested and received an immediate week's vacation. He was relieved when he wasn't asked why he suddenly needed a week off. Back in his own office, he booked the next flight to Cairo which was scheduled to leave in two hours. Not having time to go home and pack, Doyle left the police cruiser in the police department's parking lot and flagged down a taxi. He made it to DIA just in time to secure a ticket and catch his plane. He slept most of the flight, and arrived in Cairo before noon, local time. Knowing Kenny fell from a balcony at *The Ra*, Doyle decided to begin his search there and took the hotel shuttle from the airport to *The Ra*.

Doyle didn't bother to check in. He was eager to complete his *assignment* and get back to Denver. If luck was with him, he'd find Paige, eliminate her, and be back in the states before dinner time tomorrow. Approaching the desk clerk, Doyle stated in a business-like fashion, "Say, I'm meeting a representative of our foundation here. We're scheduled to attend a…a seminar together. Her name is Paige Fontaine and she's in her late twenties and stands about this tall," Doyle, remembering Paige from Margot's funeral, indicated her height with his hand. "She has dark hair and blue eyes. Perhaps you can help me?"

"Yes, sir. I know the lady you're referring to. When she doesn't stay at our sister hotel, the *Pharoah*, she stays here. However, she and her comrades checked out this morning."

Doyle was surprised when the clerk indicated Paige wasn't alone. "Comrades? Was she with someone?"

"Yes, sir. She was staying here with two gentlemen I'd never seen before."

"I see," Doyle said. "Do you know where they went?"

"Yes, sir. There was an accident last night. It occurred on Ms. Fontaine's balcony. The authorities cordoned off the entire floor and all the residents were required to relocate. I believe their party went to another one of our sister hotels—*The Desert Breeze.*"

"And the gentlemen, what did they look like?" Doyle quired.

"The American was tall and well built, the Frenchman was younger, perhaps in his twenties." Then turning the hotel register which was mounted on a carousel toward him, the clerk ran his finger down the list of hotel residents. "Here they are!" he exclaimed and turned the register back toward Doyle.

Jack Cooper! I should've known. "Thanks,

buddy," Doyle said and handed the clerk a ten spot. "Keep our conversation quiet," he said and winked. "I will and thank you, sir," the clerk said with a wide grin as he pocketed the bill.

Doyle left *The Ra* and took a taxi to *The Desert Breeze*. He was cautious not to be seen when he entered the hotel and grabbed a seat in the lobby where he had a view of all of the entrances. It was quite by chance that he glanced into the dining room and saw Jack, Paige, and Vinny seated together at a table.

• • •

The death of Kenny Clarkson was investigated by the locals and reported as a tragic accident. Paige agreed with me that getting involved in an attempted murder scandal in a foreign country was not a good idea, so we went with the accidental death theory.

Paige was scheduled to work the turn from Cairo to Paris later in the week. Although eager to get back to Paris and ultimately Savannah, Paige had to remain in Cairo the two days remaining on her three-day layover. The attempt on her life the night before resulted in the three of us agreeing to remain close together at all times.

As we lingered over brunch in *The Desert Breeze's* dining room, I mused, "I doubt I'll ever return to Egypt. And it'd be a shame not to take in some of the sights. With two days to kill, how 'bout we do some sightseeing?"

"Sure!" Vinny chirped. "I have some brochures advertising guided tours of the pyramids."

"Sounds like a once-in-a-lifetime opportunity," I replied. "And if you don't like the mystic surrounding the pyramids, there's something wrong with you." Then looking at Paige I asked, "What do you think?"

Without hesitation, Paige answered, "No thanks! Going on a tour and being exposed like a sitting duck does not appeal to me in the least. I think I'll barricade myself in my room until time to report for duty."

"Nonsense! Think about it. You'd be safer in the midst of other people," I countered. "Vinny and I will keep you safe."

Vinny nodded and took up the baton, "Come on, Ms. Paige," he coaxed. "It'll be fun."

"I suppose you'd go with or without me anyway," Paige sighed. Perhaps the thought of being left alone pushed her into making a decision. Not waiting for an answer, she reluctantly agreed to the excursion.

• • •

We purchased tickets from the tour kiosk set

up in the hotel lobby and were told the bus was in the process of loading in front of the hotel entrance. When we boarded, our bus was full of excited passengers lending a carnival-like atmosphere to the interior of our transport. The driver who spoke fluent English was a fountain of information and enlightened us with interesting facts as we traveled the eight miles from Cairo to the Pyramids of Giza.

"Ladies and gentlemen, my name is Zube, which translates in English to *comes in peace*." He then smiled and said, "Something we could all practice in today's world." I heard a few amens from the other passengers.

"You will soon view with your own eyes no less, one of the seven wonders of the ancient world. The Great Pyramid of Giza, one of the group of three which you are about to see, is the oldest of the ancient seven wonders, and the pyramids are the only ancient wonders still in existence. That, in and of itself, speaks volumes of the craftmanship involved in their erection. The pyramids are estimated to be four-thousand five-hundred years old. In comparison, let's say, if you have something that belonged to your grandmother and it's one hundred years old, it's considered an antique by today's standards and more valuable than recently purchased items. Just imagine something thousands of years old.

"You may be interested in knowing what the other six ancient wonders were. Although they are no longer in existence, they are still tributes to the ingenuity of the times. They were the Colossus of Rhodes, located on the Greek island of Rhodes; the Hanging Gardens of Babylon, located in Babil, Iraq; the Lighthouse of Alexandria, Alexandria, Egypt; the Mausoleum of Halicarnassus, Turkey; the Statute of Zeus at Olympia, Olympia, Greece; and the Temple of Artemis, also in Turkey." Zube paused, then added, "Damascus, Turkey, is thought to be the oldest continuously inhabited city in the world, and maybe that's why Turkey lays claim to two of the seven ancient wonders. It had a longer time span in which to accumulate them.

"By contrast, what are considered the new seven wonders of the world are, Chichen Itza, Mexico; Christ the Redeemer, Brazil; The Colosseum, Italy; Great Wall of China, China; Machu Picchu, Peru; and Taj Mahal, India. The Great Wall of China is the oldest of the new wonders, having commenced construction around the year three-hundred BC. The Great Pyramid, by contrast commenced construction around the year two thousand five-hundred BC. It always boggles my mind when I think that far back and wonder at the engineering feats of ancient civilizations who had only crude building implements to work with. When you see the craftsmanship associated with the pyramids, I think you, too, will be awestruck."

It was obvious my fellow passengers were as intrigued as I was by our tour guide's knowledge and rhetoric. All the passenger chatter had subsided, and no one interrupted by asking questions. As we rocked along the dusty road leading to Giza, Zube continued his spiel.

"The site we will visit is located five and a half miles west of the Nile and eight miles from Cairo." Zube jerked his thumb back in the direction of Cairo.

"The largest of the three pyramids was built for the second king of the fourth dynasty. It overshadows the other two and is known, of course, as the Great Pyramid. Some astonishing facts regarding the construction of the *Great Pyramid* are that it took over twenty years and one hundred thousand slaves to complete just that one pyramid!"

Zube scratched his beard apparently in reflection, then continued, "Food for thought, my friends. The three larger Giza pyramids combined contain two million, two hundred and fifty thousand blocks, each block weighs two hundred and fifty tons. Some speculate it would've been impossible for the ancients to have built the three large pyramids."

Vinny leaned over and whispered to me, "Even with the limestone quarry close to the construction site of the Great Pyramid, how could they load even one block weighing two hundred and fifty tons, *tons* mind you, onto an ancient transport and then move it to the site? Multiply that little operation by over two point five million blocks which, incidentally, would eventually include moving them up a ramp to the top of a four-hundred and fifty-foot-high structure, unloading them and then fitting them together almost flawlessly. Those one hundred thousand slaves must've had super-human power or help from someone with super-human power."

I marveled at Vinny's insight as I listened. *Leave it to Vinny and his analytical mind to draw that conclusion.*

If Zube overheard Vinny's comment, he didn't react. Zube continued, "By contrast in today's world, even by using modern equipment, it would take approximately fifteen hundred workers five years to build the Great Pyramid and would cost in the neighborhood of five billion dollars."

I could listen to Zube all day. He was obviously passionate about his heritage. I was almost sorry when we arrived at the site and had to leave Zube behind. Our eight-mile ride from Cairo was very enlightening, thanks to Zube, and I now looked at the pyramids with different eyes. As we exited the bus, we were greeted by several venders who had tents set up in the debussing area. Some were selling souvenirs, others were offering different forms of transportation, including jeeps and four wheelers which would be driven by Egyptian guides and used to explore the venue and travel the distances that separated the three Giza pyramids.

The most interesting form of transportation available, *if you really want to experience life on the Sahara Desert 4000 years ago* was the camel. The camel barkers' spiel was that we could rent a camel for two hours which would take us for a stroll around the pyramids for a closer look. I conferred with my companions, and since the camels didn't look all that friendly and the camel ride looked ominous, we opted to decline.

Apparently, infatuated by the idea of the ultimate adventure of a camel ride, one of our fellow passengers asked, "I'd like to try it, but what if I fall off?"

One of the camel drivers replied in perfect English, "No worries. Cleo knows her way back!" He then pointed to a camel fitted with a saddle which looked more like the seat of a child's rocking horse. It was padded with red and green throws garnished with golden-colored fringe.

"Okay, but what about me?" the persistent tourist asked as he suspiciously eyed the camel.

"Oh, in that case, I guess you're on your own," the camel driver responded and grinned.

We all indulged in a hardy laugh. And needless to say, no camels were rented that afternoon. However, because of the circumference around, and the distance between the pyramids, plus not being accustomed to the desert heat, we engaged a guide with a Jeep that didn't appear to need an attitude adjustment.

After a short ride to the site, we were escorted into the Great Pyramid by our guide, Jabari, who regaled us with a rehearsed soliloquy as we ventured into the structure.

"The Great Pyramid was built for Pharoah Khufu between two thousand five hundred and sixty and two thousand five hundred and forty BC. It contains three burial chambers, one of which was used to house the mummified body of Khufu which was entombed in a red granite sarcophagus. The other two chambers were used to store the vast amount of supplies Khufu was expected to take with him into the afterlife to tide him over until he received his eternal reward. As you can see, the chambers are now completely barren except for the red granite sarcophagus which housed the body of Khufu. Sadly enough, grave robbers emptied the chambers eons ago. It's thought that the thieves didn't waste much time after the burials to empty the tombs of the pharaohs. Competition was pretty stiff among the plunderers, so it's doubtful Khufu had a chance to take his treasurers with him to his next destination."

As we traversed the pyramid, I found it hard to concentrate and occasionally stopped and looked back expecting to see another guide and other tourists accompanying us through the pyramid. My mind kept returning to the moment when, before we entered the pyramid, I glanced out to where our Jeep was parked. Another vehicle had pulled up beside ours and the occupants, a guide and one male passenger, started toward the entrance where I stood watching. Even though the sun was in my eyes, I thought the passenger looked vaguely familiar.

"Come on," Paige called as I lagged. "Let's get on with it! Remember, this adventure was *your* idea!"

Closing the gap, I began to get an uneasy feeling and wondered how good an idea this was. I blamed my escalating uneasiness on being claustrophobic, not to mention paranoid. Encapsulated in a pyramid and not knowing how to get out didn't seem so enticing now that I was faced with the real thing.

"…and those stairs lead to an upper chamber," Jabari was saying when I approached them. In my rush to catch up, I stumbled and fell forward on the steps. Just then a bullet whizzed past my head and ricocheted off the granite wall above me. I'd been shot at before and I knew what it felt and sounded like to have a bullet fly that close to me. Paige was right in front of me, and I grabbed her and shoved her to the floor, shouting "Vinny, Jabari, get down!"

Once I was sure everyone was down, I cautiously crawled to the wall, stood, and slowly sidestepped with my back against the wall, retracing our path to this point. It didn't take long to figure out that wasn't such a good idea either when another bullet struck the granite wall within inches of my head. I froze when a male voice penetrated the passageway where I huddled.

"Cooper, play it smart. I'll let you and the kid go. All I want is the woman…"

It was then I recognized the voice. The mystery passenger I had seen before entering the pyramid was Finn Doyle. I shouted back, "Lexington must be getting desperate to send a klutz like you into the fray." I paused, concerned for his driver and the possibility of involving us in an international conflab, I asked, "What happened to your driver?"

"He's napping. Now, how 'bout we make a deal?" Doyle shouted back.

Before Doyle could outline his *deal*, Jabari was at my side. He motioned for me to follow him. The two of us pressed against the granite wall, and carefully inched along, eventually catching up with Paige and Vinny who were waiting in an alcove. Once we were united, Jabari took the lead and putting his fingers to his lips indicating for us to be quiet, he carefully ascended another flight of stone steps. We followed close behind.

"Cooper, where the hell are you?" I heard Doyle shout. His voice echoed through the pyramid's chambers.

Once again, my old buddy, claustrophobia, was beginning to close in on me. I breathed a sigh of relief when at last I saw a sliver of light penetrate the semi-darkness as we topped the staircase. Jabari motioned for us to halt. "This opening leads to the exterior of the pyramid. When we exit," he whispered, "we'll be pretty high up on the outside of the pyramid. However, there are footholds etched into the stone and it's possible to descend if you're very careful. I know the route well. I used to play here as a boy. If you follow my every move, you'll make it down just fine." Then Jabari ordered,

"Everyone take off your socks and wrap them around your palms leaving your fingers free to grip. Even though the descent takes only a few minutes, your hands will need protection from the extremely hot rocks."

I glanced at Paige. She stared daggers at me as she said, "I was just joking about my bucket list…"

Her sense of humor reassured me, and I replied, "I promise this won't be the last entry on your bucket list."

"Cooper!" Doyle shouted again. Much to my distress, he sounded closer. He most likely found the stairs and was hot on our trail.

The four of us crawled out of the interior of the pyramid. Jabari arranged our exit so that he was in the lead, and he had already begun the descent. As we followed, we must've looked like four monkeys backing down a stepladder. Vinny was at the top, Paige was in line beneath him, I was below Paige and Jabari was leading the way carefully down the pyramid, step-by-step.

"Hey, boss, this is pretty cool," Vinny said as we descended the blistering hot stones. "Just don't look down—or up!" he cautioned.

I hate heights and didn't need to be reminded. I was also *blessed* with acrophobia as well as claustrophobia and began to wish I'd listened to

Paige before embarking on this excursion. We were making good progress, and so far, there were no heart-stopping incidents, either figuratively or literally. My nerves were jangling as I wondered where Doyle was, so I glanced up. *Damnit!* There he was closing the gap between us. He had found the passage and the opening and was following us down the pyramid, at a pretty good clip I might add. I didn't alert the others for fear they would try to hurry and get careless. A fall would mean instant death.

I was startled when a loose rock tumbled past fairly close to us. Vinny must've looked up and spotted Doyle when the rock fell. "Hey, boss—" he shouted.

Before he could say more, I cut him off. "I know," I shouted back. "Just keep moving." I was eager to get the descent behind us, so I asked Jabari in anxious anticipation, "How much further?"

Still working his way downward, and without looking up at me, Jabari responded, "About two stories in building parlance. That would be around twenty feet or so in layman's terms. However, this route takes us to the top of the sphinx at the entrance of the Great Pyramid."

"Okay," I shouted. "Then what?"

"From the head of the sphinx it's another

couple of stories to ground level. The good news is the stairs are inside the sphinx. The tricky part is getting inside of the head."

"I don't want to know the details," I again shouted. "You've done a great job so far, so you just lead the way, and we'll follow."

We remained silent the remainder of the descent. When we got to the sphinx, Jabari suddenly disappeared, apparently in the inside of the sphinx's head. After a moment, he stuck his head out of the opening, and ordered, "Do exactly as I tell you." And reaching for me, he extended his hand. "Give me your hand!" he ordered.

The two remaining stories didn't sound like much but when I looked down, I became queasy. My heart wasn't in it, but I did as I was told. Jabari was much stronger than he looked and as he held my hand firmly in his grasp, he jerked me into the interior of the sphinx in one fell swoop. I landed on my knees on the stone floor. By the time I got to my feet, Jabari was coaxing Paige. I went to the opening and could see the fear in her eyes. "Paige," I yelled. "Take Jabari's hand. If you slip, I'll grab you."

Probably too frightened to speak, Paige obeyed and took Jabari's hand. When he had a tight grip on her, Jabari reached out with his other hand, and grabbing her arm, whisked her inside the sphinx's head. We followed the same procedure with Vinny and soon all of us were safely inside the sphinx.

Thankful that we were all safe, at least for the moment, I shouted, "We don't have any time to waste. Doyle is right behind us."

Paige, who was sitting on the stone steps, exclaimed, "Oh, no!" and jumped up. She turned and started her descent.

"Hold on, lady!" Jabari ordered. "I'll take the lead." "It's still dangerous. Some of the steps have deteriorated…"

The passage was dark and narrow, and we lined up again. This time I brought up the rear.

"Cooper! You sorry bastard…" Doyle shouted. It sounded as though he was fairly close to the sphinx's head.

"Let's go!" I said to Jabari and the four of us headed down the stone steps of the poorly lit interior of the sphinx.

We had to do a couple of hand-over-hand maneuvers when we came to the places where steps were missing but the descent was nothing like the one down the side of the pyramid. Reaching the bottom, we rushed out into the sunlight. Paige immediately fell to her knees and buried her face in her hands, either exhausted or in grateful prayer to the one living and true God—maybe both.

We were unable to take time to recuperate, so we headed for our Jeep *posthaste*. When we approached, I noticed the buses and all the other tourists had already left. Even the four-wheeler Doyle arrived in was gone. The guide/driver probably woke up from his nap and decided to hell with his lunatic passenger and left without him. *Hope Doyle enjoys the eight-mile hike back to Cairo.*

Chapter Eight

Panic on the Potomac

"Lexington, I'm in the hospital here in Cairo," Doyle stammered as soon as the senator answered his private line.

"Why? What happened?" snapped Lexington.

"Sunstroke!" Then Doyle proceeded to relate to Lexington the sequence of events that occurred in Cairo. "I followed them when they left the hotel and—"

"Them?" Lexington interrupted.

"Yeah, she was with Jack Cooper. You know the PI that Margot went to see—"

"Yeah, yeah. I know. What happened?" Lexington asked in an anxious voice.

"Well, we all took an in-depth tour of the pyramids—including crawling down the blistering hot stone outside of the Great Pyramid."

"The outside? How in hell's name—"

"Don't speak to me about hell…been there! The long and the short of it is they got away and I ended up in the hospital."

"How'd that happen?" Lexington asked.

"While I was crawling around the pyramids,

my driver left me stranded in the desert. I had to walk eight miles back to Cairo. On my way back, I was on the verge of collapse when I was picked up by one of the camel drivers. He basically saved my life. My lips were so parched they had cracked open, and my mouth was so dry, I could spit cotton. The camel driver had a canteen of water and he offered it to me. Even though it tasted like warm camel pee, I drank every drop. He then ordered one of the camels to kneel. After helping me up on its back, he brought me to Cairo where I'm hospitalized with sunstroke."

"On a camel?" Lexington asked.

"Yes, on the back of a camel. Believe me, that's something you don't ever want to experience. Kudos to those tough souls who ride camels every day. My insides feel like they've been in a blender."

After a long silence, Lexington remarked sarcastically, "So we're back where we started, only worse off than before, right?"

"Right."

"How long before you're released?" Lexington asked.

"Probably not until tomorrow," said Doyle. Moments passed before he added, "I've pretty much had it and I'm not going back to Denver. I phoned the department today and resigned and now

I'm advising you that I'm no longer your minion!"

"What! You can't do that. With Kenny dead and now you quitting, that leaves me with basically nobody I can depend on. What…what are you going to do?"

"Donno yet, but I'll find something less stressful. Tired of chasing, being chased, shooting at people and being shot at, crawling around on pyramids…" Doyle muttered, then added, "If my trek across the desert was a preview of hell, count me out. I'm changing my ways." After a moment of silence, he added, "You may want to consider doing the same." Doyle then hung up the phone without saying goodbye.

After the call ended so abruptly, Lexington sat at his desk staring straight ahead, focusing on nothing. He rose from his desk and went to the window of his senate office where he could see the Potomac River peacefully winding its way to the Atlantic. Everything appeared to be the same, but his world was quickly collapsing. Being a United States senator was one of his lifetime ambitions as was his being groomed by his party to run for president in the upcoming general election. Now his aspirations were close to being destroyed by Paige Fontaine. Although he was alone in his office, he couldn't control his temper and began raging.

In his now patented fury, he shouted, cursed, and pounded his desk. His obscenities were directed at Paige, Doyle, Kenny, the Sabenese, and everyone else who was interfering with his future. He was known for having a terrible temper, but this outburst was violent to the point of being scary.

When his secretary timidly tapped on his door and asked if he was alright, he realized his actions weren't just confined to his inner office.

"Sorry, Stella. Yes, I'm alright," he managed to utter as he tried desperately to control his raging temper.

"Do you still want me to hold your calls?" she asked.

"Depends. Whose calling?"

"Ammon, Sahib Abakali's secretary. He said it was urgent he talk with you."

Urgent? Now what? "Okay, put him through," Lexington ordered. When his phone rang, Lexington yanked it up. "Ammon!" he said in a contrived voice. "I was just going to call the Sahib."

"Then, I take it, you have some good news to report?" Ammon asked.

"Ah, not yet. We're still working out the details—"

"Details? What details? "The Sahib would like to forward a favorable report to Shambu Oman on the progress you're making concerning the agreement between you and our nation. The Sahib was under the impression as soon as you were sworn in as senator, you'd have the deal secured," Ammon snapped. After a pause, he asked, "Now, what do I tell him?"

"Ah…let him know everything is proceeding according to schedule and not to worry. I'll be in touch," Lexington said and hung up the phone before he could be bombarded with more questions he couldn't answer. Sweat dripped from Lexington's brow as he thought of the consequences in the event of his inability to keep his promises—especially to Sahib Abakali.

• • •

Being cut off so abruptly, especially by an infidel, was considered a slap in the face, so to speak. Ammon immediately reported his abrupt conversation with Lexington to the Sahib. After hearing the details, and that Lexington basically cut Ammon off by hanging up on him, the Sahib rubbed the back of his neck in thoughtful reflection. He then told Ammon to make preparations for a trip to the United States as soon as possible. It was obvious to Ammon that the Sahib's patience was rapidly dissipating.

"Much is not right with that one. He's being

very illusive. The Shambu would expect that we go and personally determine what's going on," Sahib Abakali said. "I do not trust the Americans. I personally guaranteed the reliability of Lexington to the Shambu. We invested millions of U.S. dollars getting that infidel elected upon his assurance the oil deal we discussed would be a shoo-in once he was sworn in. Now, by Allah, he's going to keep his part of the arrangement! It's either his head or mine!"

• • •

It's a known fact that when you hold the position of Sahib, the wheels turn fast and the next day the Sahib's personal jet taxied up to the terminal at Dulles International Airport. The Sabenese were granted diplomatic immunity and not required to make any declarations upon their arrival in the United States, so a prearranged limo was waiting on the tarmac to transport Sahib Abakali, Ammon, and two bodyguards to Senator Lexington's office.

• • •

Stella almost dropped her coffee cup when the Saudi entourage burst into Senator Lexington's office suite and marched up to her desk. They were dressed in traditional Arab garb. Their white robes flowed as they walked, and they all wore a red and white checkered Keffiyeh headdress secured to the top of their heads with a thick black band. "They had fire in their eyes, and I was terrified," she would later relate to one of the senator's aids.

"Please announce Sahib Abakali is here to see Senator Lexington," Ammon ordered.

"Yes, sir," Stella stuttered, and her hands trembled as she fumbled with the intercom. Her eyes were riveted on the sabers the bodyguards wore. The Sahib was not accustomed to waiting and it appeared he wanted to *surprise* the senator. After waiting a few moments for Stella to announce his presence, he said, "Never mind! I'll do it myself." He then motioned to his men who were positioned by the entrance to follow him. Sahib Abakali closed the distance between Stella's desk and Lexington's office door in literally seconds with his entourage close behind.

Lexington was seated behind his desk. His life was beginning to unravel, and in his present state of mind, when his door banged open, he jumped up and rounded his desk with clinched fists with rage in his eyes. It was apparent he was ready for a fight. "What in the hell do you think you're doing? You can't just barge…" he began.

Standing in the open doorway, Abakali looked back over his shoulder at his men and sneered, "I respectfully disagree, it appears that we *can just barge in here!"*

The fire in Lexington's eyes changed to unmistakable fear when he came face-to-face with Abakali. Abakali pushed past Lexington, seated himself in Lexington's leather chair, and promptly propped his feet up on Lexington's desk. He picked up Lexington's letter opener and proceeded to clean his fingernails. Then, pointing to one of the chairs positioned on the other side of the desk, Abakali said, "Take a seat, *my friend.*" It sounded more like a command than a request and Lexington complied. With the soles of Abakali's sandals facing him, Lexington obviously understood the significance of the gesture. In Sabenialand, positioning the soles of one's shoes in someone else's face was the ultimate insult.

It was apparent Lexington had also noticed the bodyguards' sabers. As he slowly lowered himself onto one of the chairs, he asked, "How'd they get weapons in here?"

Glancing back at the door at the three men standing military rigid with their hands on the hilt of their sabers, Abakali replied, "*Diplomatic immunity*! My bodyguards' weapons are for my protection. I noticed on the drive here from the airport there were many uniformed soldiers stationed in and around the U.S. Capitol Building and they all were carrying automatic weapons. So, what's the difference. Is your protection more important than mine?"

Although Sahib Abakali was not a diplomat, he must have pull somewhere, so Lexington let the matter drop and remained silent. Anyway, he had more urgent issues to contend with. His mind was racing trying to come up with a plausible reason for the delay in the execution and implementation of the all-important oil transaction between the Sabenese and the United States that he was supposed to be brokering through his committee and subcommittee assignments.

"You know why I'm here!" Abakali exclaimed with determination in his voice.

"Yes."

"And…"

Having previously spent hours wrestling with the problem, it apparently occurred to Lexington when he was unable to conjure up a believable story that perhaps, like his mother taught without any real success, *Honesty is the best policy!* Plus, he knew how the Sabenese viewed women, and hopefully the Sahib would understand why Margot had to be eliminated and not judge him too harshly. Time would tell! And the proverb that a *A man is in charge of his own destiny* no doubt was foremost in Lexington's mind. If it wasn't then, it soon would be!

Glancing again at the trio standing guard at his door, Lexington said in an almost apologetic tone, "I have something very personal to tell you." Nodding toward Ammon and the two bodyguards, he asked, "Is it necessary for them to be in here?"

Abakali paused cleaning his nails momentarily and looked up. Then, without a moment's hesitation, replied, "Yes, it *is* necessary! Please go on."

Taking a deep breath, Lexington related to Abakali how and why he killed Margot. He borrowed a page from the pilot's manual. Blame the crash on co-pilot error! "I don't know how she found out about the deal I had with you, but I couldn't trust her not to disclose it and bring down the house of cards. She had to be eliminated."

"I see," said Abakali. "So, with the elimination of Margot, we can now proceed?"

Lexington was visibly uncomfortable as he continued. "I found out later Margot forwarded a video of me to her sister, Paige, just as I pulled the trigger. She had been sending poses to Paige modeling her new sunglasses and was on the phone prior to and at the time of the shooting. Paige now has the video in her possession and if she turns it over to the authorities, my goose is cooked."

"I see," Abakali said and tossed the letter opener onto Lexington's desk. "However, I don't understand why she would continue to send videos if she realized you were about to shoot her!" he said with skepticism evident from the tone of his voice.

"Margot didn't actually see me. Apparently, the sunglasses captured the reflection of me approaching and shooting her. Her phone picked up the scene and forwarded the video to Paige in real time."

"Real time?"

"Yes, real time means just as the event is taking place."

"I see."

"Paige and I were never close even though I was her brother-in-law. I was always under the impression she didn't like me. I couldn't and can't chance the possibility that Paige would or will turn the evidence over to the authorities and that the video obviously would be the smoking gun should the authorities file murder charges."

"Understood," Abakali responded.

In for a penny, in for a pound, Lexington thought and took a deep breath as he continued. "Another concern was and is, if I follow through with our arrangement and if I'm arrested for murder, your country could possibly be involved in an international scandal." Lexington hoped he would get some points for showing his concern for someone other than himself, even if it was contrived.

"So, now where is the video?" Abakali asked with piqued interest.

"I destroyed Margot's cellphone after I shot her. At that time, I didn't realize that Paige had the video also on her cellphone. She's an *Egyptian Skies* flight attendant and is hard to catch up with. I've lost two men trying to retrieve *her* cellphone."

After a long pause, Abakali said, "Hmm, perhaps we can be of assistance. Persuasion where I come from can take on many forms. I have connections with the airlines and can find out where she is and her travel schedule. We can take it from here."

On the way out the door, Abakali paused and looking back at Lexington. asked, "Where can we send the flowers?"

"Send flowers?" a perplexed Lexington asked hoping Abakali's motives for asking were for noble purposes.

"For your casket in case everything fails!" Abakali said matter-of-factly and shrugged. He bid Lexington ado with a swipe of the hand across his neck—a gesture meant to invoke intimidation and fear.

Chapter Nine

Full Circle

I booked reservations for Vinny and me on the *Egyptian Skies* flight Paige was assigned to, and we headed back to Paris. After the Cairo/Paris turn, Paige had a five-day hiatus. She was able to call ahead and get reservations for her and me on a *Delta* flight from Paris to Savannah. When we arrived at the *Charles de Gaulle* airport in Paris, before we parted ways, we said our goodbyes to Vinny.

"Hey, boss, being your *interpreter* was the most excitement and fun I've ever had. *Thanks for the memories!*" Vinny said and snapped to attention giving me a smart salute.

I watched Paige roll her eyes in mock disgust. "In that case," she said, "I don't want to know what you consider life-threatening trauma and just plain terror."

"Ah, come on, Ms. Paige. Admit it! How many people can brag about descending the outside of *the* Great Pyramid and crawling around inside the head of a sphinx while being shot at by a hired assassin," Vinny teased.

"Not many, and I wish I weren't one of them,"

Paige replied.

When we reached the Delta waiting area, we exchanged hugs all around. "And Vinny," I said, "having you as my *interpreter* was one of the highlights of my life. You take care and keep in touch."

"Will do, boss. And you do the same," he said as he shouldered his duffel bag.

We watched Vinny proceeded to the exit, but before he was out of sight, he turned and waved. I waved back and Paige blew him a kiss. He reached up and grabbed the imaginary kiss and pressed his clinched fist containing the imaginary kiss to his heart.

Turning toward the ticket counter, I teasingly remarked, "You Parisians are so melodramatic."

"We call it *romantic!* You Americans could take lessons!" Paige quipped.

Is that an invitation? I pondered and smiled.

• • •

"I have a second bedroom," Paige said as we were preparing to land in Savannah. "You're welcome to use it until you return to Denver."

I'd been watching Paige closely. She appeared to be nervous and jumped at every little noise. Her jitters, plus the comments about *just plain terror*, were red flags. I think the events of the last three days had taken their toll and she no longer felt secure being alone.

"That's very kind of you," I responded. "However, it would be a short stay. I've booked a flight and will be leaving Savannah tomorrow morning." When her face fell and her expression changed to disappointment, especially after being so optimistic only moments before, I had an epiphany. "Why don't you fly to Denver with me and stay at least until your next assignment. I, too, have a spare bedroom."

"That's very kind of you," she said and smiled, and relief was evident in her voice. "I accept your offer."

After clearing the airport in Savannah, we took a taxi to Paige's apartment and I carried our bags into the building and waited as Paige inserted her door key into the lock.

"That's funny," she replied with a perplexed expression on her face. "The door doesn't seem to be locked—"

I put my finger to my lips signaling for her to be silent and gently edged her aside. Motioning for her to stay low, I bent down and retrieved my gun from my duffel. Pressing myself against the wall, I nudged the door open with my foot careful not to be an easy target. The interior of her apartment was dark and still.

"You stay put while I do some recon," I whispered. Paige nodded. After a few minutes, I returned to the open door. "No one here," I said. "But your place has been thoroughly ransacked."

"Oh, no!" Paige exclaimed when she entered and saw the condition of her condo. She slumped down on the sofa which, incidentally, had all the cushions slit open, and buried her face in her hands. "Why would anyone want to do this?" she murmured.

"Looks like the work of someone desperate to find the video," I replied.

When I mentioned *video*, Paige jumped up and immediately went to her computer. The monitor and keyboard were shattered. "The culprits messed up my computer. However, it looks like the CPU hasn't been breached. I don't think they were able to hack into my data. Hopefully, *Ricochet* is still intact." Then patting her pocket, Paige said, "Even if they did, at least we still have the video on my iPhone."

The shock of having her home burglarized, seemed to have increased Paige's paranoia. She walked from room to room wringing her hands and shaking her head. I was afraid to leave her alone. The flight to Denver left Savannah at 7:30

a.m. and since there was nothing we could do to rectify the condition of her apartment, I suggested we overnight in a hotel close to the airport. The strong, sassy Paige I knew now trembled and clung tightly to my arm as we left her apartment building. Her voice was weak, and she stuttered from time-to-time when she spoke.

• • •

When we got to our room, I was so exhausted, I collapsed on one of the beds and fell into a deep sleep. Paige must've slept pretty well, too. We were up early enough to indulge in the hotel's Continental breakfast. Since we hadn't eaten anything since leaving Paris the day before, I was ravenous. Bacon, eggs, and hotcakes never tasted so good.

Paige appeared to be in better spirits and more like her old self. "I apologize for being such a wimp last night when I saw my apartment," she said as she smeared cream cheese on a bagel. "It's not like me. We're trained to stay calm and cope with emergency situations, and… and I think I flunked the test."

"Not at all. In fact, you held up exceptionally well considering the accumulation of earth-shattering events over the last three days. Look at you now—you bounce back pretty well!"

Paige blushed as she bit into the bagel.

· · ·

Apparently, having been scared out of her wits by two attempts on her life, Paige was now even more anxious to get the video into the hands of the authorities. The first thing I did when we arrived in Denver was to contact Thornton. However, since his partner, Finn Doyle, tried to kill us in Cairo, I proceeded with caution not knowing on which side Thornton had aligned himself.

"Hey, Thornton," I said when he answered his phone. Appearing to be casual to throw him off guard in the event he was on Lexington's payroll, I asked, "What's new?"

"Hell, man. Where've you been? Tried to contact you a number of times."

"Been out of the country on a job," I replied.

"That figures. Well, *what's new* is that Doyle just up and resigned. No reason. He took some vacation time and about a week later called the chief and said *adiós*."

Still playing dumb, I said, "That's odd. Any idea where he went on vacation?"

"None whatsoever. Even though we were partners, we didn't socialize much. We weren't that close, and he didn't confide in me. Since he wasn't married, we had different interests and after work, went our separate ways. He spent a lot of time in singles bars currying favor with the unattached females who were fascinated with cops. However, interestingly enough, Collins just returned from a week in Hawaii. He said he thought he saw Doyle in Maui lounging under a canopy on the patio of the hotel where Collins was staying. Collins said the guy he thought was Doyle was seated with a foxy chick sipping one of those fancy drinks they serve with miniature umbrellas. Said the fellow had a full beard but he could tell he was pretty tan, like he'd spent a lot of time in the sun or was just recovering from a sunburn. Collins said that since he couldn't be sure it was Doyle, and didn't recognize the chick, he didn't speak not wanting to look like a fool if he was mistaken."

"Hmm. So, you haven't heard from Doyle since he jumped ship?" I asked engaging on a fishing expedition to find out if Thornton was on Lexington's payroll and in cahoots with Doyle.

"Nope. Not a word," he replied. "Like I said, we weren't that close." After a pause, Thornton added, "But you'd think being his partner, he would've said something and not just drop off the end of the earth."

I looked at Paige and gave her a thumbs up indicating that I thought I could trust Thornton. She nodded, so I turned my attention back to

Thornton. "I have a situation I'd like to run past you, but I don't want to come to the station. How 'bout lunch?" I asked and quickly added, "My turn to buy."

"Okay. With all the strange things that have been happening, I'm very curious about what's going on," Thornton responded. "But, just to show I'm not a vindictive person, even though you're buying, I'd prefer the seven-dollar burgers at *Red Robin*. Meet you there at one."

He was of course slamming me for the $15 burgers I stuck him with the last time we had lunch, so I let it pass without comment.

When we arrived at the restaurant, Thornton was already seated. He stood as we approached the table and held a chair for Paige. "Afternoon, Ms. Fontaine," he said. "Nice to see you again." Thornton offered me his hand across the table and his quizzical look said *what's she doing here?*

As soon as we were seated, I cut to the chase. "Paige has decided to turn over to you the cellphone with the video incriminating Lexington. After my initial conversation with you, two attempts were made on Paige's life in Cairo. In one incident, the would-be assassin accidentally died instead."

Thornton raised his brow but before he could ask another question, our waitress appeared. After taking our order, she retreated and I continued, "When the first attempt on Paige's life failed, Doyle suddenly showed up in Cairo—"

"What! You're kidding. Finn Doyle went to Cairo!" a surprised Thornton exclaimed. "Cairo, Egypt?"

"Yep! Not Cairo, Illinois," I said. "Not only did he travel to Cairo, he, too, attempted to kill Paige… and me and a couple of others in the process."

"What! I…I don't believe it!" Thornton stammered. "Finn Doyle of all people. I was his partner for six years and never saw that side of him. Are you sure it was him?"

"Yes, I'm sure our would-be assassin was Finn Doyle. Remember, I'm personally acquainted with him and would recognize him on sight," I said. "He must've been Lexington's mole in the department and when you told him about the incriminating video, he forwarded the info to Lexington. After Doyle showed up in Cairo, I put two-and-two together and figured Lexington ordered him to retrieve the evidence and get rid of the source. I just happened to be in the vicinity when the attempts were made on Paige's life."

"Well, I'll be…" Thornton said and furrowed his brow. "So, if the fellow Collins saw was Doyle, how'd he end up in Maui?"

"Long story, but for now we need to concentrate on the present and provide protection for Paige. When we returned from Cairo, her place had been tossed. I don't see Lexington giving up even after two failed attempts on Paige's life, and it appears he will stop at nothing to get the video. You can imagine that if Lexington had a couple of killers on his payroll as mayor, I'm sure his status as senator and the money and power behind him has made working for him even more desirable. Needless to say, Paige's life is in jeopardy."

Thornton nodded. After recovering from the initial shock of learning his partner was a hired assassin, it appeared he was finally grasping the situation. "Does she have the video with her now?" he asked.

I looked at Paige. By way of answering Thornton's question, Paige dug around in her oversized handbag and retrieved her iPhone. Probably relieved to be rid of it, she handed it to Thornton without hesitation. He stared at it for a moment, as if unable to believe he finally had the evidence he needed to arrest Lexington for first degree murder. He then secured it in his jacket pocket.

"When I get back to the station, I'll have the lab guys examine this. If they can make the connection with Senator Lexington, then all hell's going to break loose." After a brief pause, he added, "We'll be making duplicates of the video and securing them where a select few have access."

I nodded then asked, "And how about protection for Paige?"

"I'll take care of that, too," Thornton promised. "I'll assign an around-the-clock team until we sort this out." Then looking at Paige, he asked, "Where are you staying?"

"With Jack for the time being. I only have five days off before I report back to duty and I'll be leaving the country," Paige replied. "Do you think it will take longer than that to make the arrest?"

"Well, I'm pretty sure we know where to find the senator. If he doesn't get wind that we may have enough evidence to arrest him, I'm certain he won't run. His inflated ego and political aspirations would probably compel him to stay and fight. After we view the video, and if the evidence is as you claim, I'll immediately contact the DA and obtain an arrest warrant for Lexington. I've worked with the DA for a number of years and have never doubted his dedication in seeing that justice is served. He's not one who can be intimidated or bought off." And while still directing his attention to Paige, Thornton added, "I think once he's in custody on murder charges, you'll be safe enough. Although you'll probably be called as a witness, the video will speak for itself, and there will be no need for him to commit another murder to add to the body count—and extend his prison sentence or risk the death penalty."

• • •

After lunch, the three of us split up in the parking lot. Paige and I headed to my place and Thornton left for the police department. I was in slumber land when sometime after midnight my phone rang startling me awake.

"'Lo," I said in a sleepy voice.

"Jack, it's Thornton."

"Yeah! What's up?" I asked. Still half asleep, I sat up on the edge of the bed as something in my head said that this couldn't be good news at this hour. I looked up and saw Paige standing in my bedroom doorway. She must've heard the phone ring. I motioned her in and put the phone on speaker so she could hear the conversation.

"I'm in the hospital. Been diagnosed with a concussion. I was blindsided when I got back to the station. Two thugs jumped me in the parking lot." Thornton paused, then said, "Jack, they got the cellphone."

"Oh, my God!" I exclaimed. "Are *you* going to

be okay?"

"Think so. They want to keep me here until tomorrow for observation." Thornton sounded pretty miserable when he added, "Sorry, buddy. They must've been watching when we did the exchange at the restaurant."

"Not your fault. Just concentrate on getting better," I said. "I'll be in touch."

Paige sat down on the bed beside me. "Jack," she said, "I'm a geek and I have an idea."

"You're a what?" I blurted.

"You know, one of those people who love computers and all the technology that goes with them. We're referred to by the general population as geeks."

"I'm embarrassed to admit that I know very little about computers," I confessed. "Consider me a novice!"

Paige seemed undeterred. "By keeping up on the latest trends in technology," she continued, "I think, if my CPU is undamaged, I can access it by using your computer. The program is called *Fast Remote Access* and I've been reading up on it. The claim is you can access your personal computer by using another computer from any location in the world."

"You're kidding!" I again exclaimed. "What will they think of next?" Then after a pause, I asked, "So all is not lost?"

"Absolutely not!" Paige said emphatically. "Since your computer isn't damaged, I think I can hack into my secondary storage device. It's a hard drive that holds all files, programs, music and movies. I haven't tried it yet, but…come on, what'd we have to lose? Let's use your computer and give it a try," she urged.

I admired her confidence and spunk—even if she was a *geek*. Once we were seated at my computer, Paige flexed her fingers and asked, "Okay, what's your password?"

Oh, no! I sank lower in my chair and hesitated. Positioning her fingers over the keyboard, she peered at me and persisted, "Jack, what's your password?"

Even more embarrassed, I groaned. I never thought I'd have to disclose my password to anyone, and now, seeing no way around it, I mumbled, "Bondjamesbond007."

Paige turned and looked at me and with a wide grin, and said, "You wish!"

I wrestled down my humiliation as I watched Paige manipulate the keyboard. After a few minutes of hits and misses, Paige shouted, *"Voila!* I've got it, Jack, I've got it!" She moved aside to give me room and proceeded to play the video on my computer for me to view. Seeing it on a bigger and better screen, I could clearly tell the shooter was indeed our infamous Senator Leonard Lexington.

I reached over and gave her a big hug, and to my delight, she hugged me back. "Paige, you're a...a *geek's geek*. Good job!"

"Thank you. That's quite a compliment. Besides, I owe it to Margot," Paige said in a soft voice, obviously still mourning over the loss of her sister. When the moment passed, she clamored, "Now, double-o-seven, let's nail that bastard!"

REFLECTION OF A KILLER — JUDITH BLEVINS & CARROLL MULTZ

Chapter Ten

The Best Laid Plans...

As was his habit of late, Sahib Abakali, along with his entourage burst into Lexington's office without being announced. Although Lexington was once again incensed by the lack of respect shown him by the Sabenese, his disposition soon changed when Abakali slid a cellphone across his desk. Rounding Lexington's desk, Abakali sat down on the corner, and pointed to the cellphone, "Here's the item you requested," he said with a grin.

Lexington just stared at the cellphone for long moments, apparently trying to grasp the realization that it was at last in his possession. He finally picked it up and turning it over in his hands he examined it. He noticed the exterior case was pretty well scratched up. He made no attempt to engage the contents. Still looking at the phone and unable to keep his voice from quivering, he asked Abakali in a subdued voice, "Have you viewed the video?"

"I have."

"And?"

"It clearly depicts you shooting your wife!" Abakali stated matter-of-factly without even a hint of compassion in his voice.

If Lexington was shocked by the revelation and Abakali's lack of respect, it didn't show. Lexington just nodded but still made no attempt to engage the video.

"Here," Abakali said, and his voice conveyed impatience. "Let me help you." He then took the cellphone from Lexington's hands. Scrolling through the screens, he finally found the incriminating segment and handed the phone back to Lexington. Pointing with his index finger, he said, "Just press that button to start the show."

When Lexington didn't respond, Abakali sighed, "Oh, you Americans. You're so squeamish. Since you haven't the guts to look for yourself, just take my word for it."

"She…she was my wife, after all," Lexington whispered.

"In my country anyone and everyone is expendable, especially disobedient wives. They know they can be replaced with a snap of the fingers, so they seldom break the rules. You Americans are too lenient and by giving them equal rights…well that's your country's problem." After a pause, he added, "Speaking of which, now that your problem is solved, would it be possible to move forward with our deal?"

Eager for Abakali to leave his office, Lexington said, "Yes. I'll start the process at our next committee meeting."

"And I'll hold you to that promise," Abakali stated, and the veiled threat was unmistakable. He then motioned for his entourage to follow him out. Before clearing Lexington's office, he turned, and with his patented gesture, swiped his hand across his neck.

After the Sabenese left his office, Lexington rested his head against the high back of his leather chair and closed his eyes. *The good news is I'm now in possession of the video. The bad news is what if the committee continues to resist and I'm unable to fulfill my end of the deal with the Sabenese. They wouldn't dare kill a United States senator—would they?*

• • •

Paige and I sat for long moments huddled together in front of my computer. I still could scarcely believe she was able to retrieve the video from the trashed debris that was once her computer. I marveled at the technical advances achieved in the twentieth century but was in awe of those who could implement them—sometimes by only using bobby pins, chewing gum and lots of grit.

Paige broke the silence. "Where do we go from

here?" she asked.

"I've been thinking about that," I responded. "The experience we had with Doyle has shaken my confidence in the police department. Thornton's still in the hospital, and I wouldn't trust anyone else with the video or even let anyone else know we have it, and at this point, not even the DA! Thornton said he'd be out of the hospital in a day or so, but even then, after suffering a concussion, he may not be up to par—mentally or physically."

Looking pensive, Paige said poignantly, "Jack, I can't hide forever. Since they think they have the only evidence, do you feel I'm still in danger?"

I thought about Paige's question for a moment, and finally responded, "Not really. Their mindset may be, that without any corroborating evidence, your word that there is a video wouldn't hold much water in a court of law, especially since Lexington thinks you can't produce it. He probably thinks that no DA in his right mind would bring charges and no judge would go up against a United States senator on the say-so of a victim's disgruntled sister. Even the DA would probably consider your accusations sour grapes." After a brief pause, I continued, "So to answer your question specifically, killing you would serve no purpose, except perhaps to draw more attention to Margot's unsolved murder—

which I guarantee Lexington wouldn't want to do."

"That makes sense," Paige said reflectively. "Then, if you think it's safe, I'll leave tomorrow. I must get back to Paris for my next Cairo turn. However, there's no way I'm going to chance going back to my apartment in Savannah. I'll phone the landlord before I leave here. Under the circumstances, I'm hopeful he'll waive the remainder of my lease. The furniture in the apartment that was mine is in shambles and not worth salvaging. I'll ask him to dispose of it and box up my personal items which I'll arrange to pick up later. Fortunately, I always carry an extra uniform with me. You never know when a passenger might get air sick and… well, you know what."

I nodded and said, "I can only guess but spare me the details. Besides, looking normal will work to our advantage. Since Lexington and his merry band of killers believe you no longer have the cellphone, I think you'll be safe enough. He's probably reveling in the thought that there now isn't an iota of evidence against him and he's as free as a bird. I'll keep an eye on Thornton and if I feel he's up to it, I'll forward the video to him."

"Un-huh," Paige said. "I've seen your computer skills, and *double oh seven*, even though you've been known to disarm nuclear weapons in ten seconds or less, I'm not so sure you wouldn't accidentally delete the video."

"That bad, huh?" I said reliving my embarrassment and hoping my silly password wasn't going to haunt me the rest of my natural life.

"Yep," Paige said with a smile. "But I have an idea. I found an unopened thumb drive in your desk drawer. I could download the video onto it. A thumb drive is small and discrete and will fit into the palm of your hand. All you'd have to do is press it into Thornton's hand when you exchange handshakes next time you see him. If you're very careful, no one will be the wiser. That way, you wouldn't have to worry about transmitting it electronically and taking a chance on erasing it. Plus, we'd still have a copy on your computer in case something else unexpected happens."

"Not only are you a geek, but you're also a genius!" I said and shot her my most ingratiating smile. I was disappointed when it appeared that she didn't seem to notice and went nonchalantly about the business of loading the video onto the thumb drive. *Must be losing my touch.*

My fears were in vain. Later that night I was awakened when Paige nudged me over and slipped into bed beside me. I took her in my arms and pulled her close. No words were necessary.

• • •

The next morning, I took Paige to DIA where she deadheaded a flight to Paris. She was scheduled to be gone a week. I wasn't allowed to accompany her any further than the check-in lane. After she showed her ID and was approved to proceed through, we stepped aside to say our goodbyes. When she could stall no longer, I gathered her to me and gently kissed her. Her return kiss said more than just goodbye.

"I'll be here waiting for you," I whispered.

"And I'll count the minutes until we're back together," she responded. Then she pulled away from me and headed down the concourse toward her flight. But before she was out of sight, she turned and waved. I blew her the quintessential kiss. Smiling, she imitated Vinny and grabbed the *kiss* out of the air and pressed to her heart. She then disappeared from view and I headed for the exit. As I left DIA, I couldn't remember when I'd ever felt this good. Even the pandemonium of DIA and the Denver traffic didn't affect me, I was on *cloud nine!*

• • •

During her absence, I planned to surreptitiously provide Thornton with the thumb drive. When I learned Thornton had been released from the hospital, I wasn't sure if he was back in his office yet, so I called him on his cellphone.

"Thornton here," he answered.

"Are you home or at the office," I asked, relieved to hear his voice.

"Who wants to know?" he growled.

"It's Jack!"

"Oh, didn't recognize your voice. Thought it may be one of the thugs lining up a repeat performance." A moment later Thornton said, "I'm at work. After I was released from the hospital, I couldn't stand the stay-at-home boredom and the wife doting on me all the time, so I came back to work. What's your status?"

"Looking for a lunch companion."

"You just found one. *Chews*, twenty minutes."

Even though the opposition couldn't know Paige was able to download a copy of the video from her home computer, I didn't dare mention the thumb drive for fear his phone could be tapped. I'd just have to be the PI I purport to be and skillfully slip him the device when we shook hands.

When Thornton entered, I stood and extended my hand. "Good to see you looking so fit. You had us worried for a while," I said, and as I grasped his right hand with both of mine, I pressed the thumb drive into his right palm. He looked confused for an instant but apparently realizing I was transferring something to him, he didn't react.

"You know what they say about old soldiers," he replied as he sat down and ceremoniously removed his glasses from his breast jacket pocket. He must've slipped the thumb drive into the pocket as he removed the glasses because when he picked up his menu, his right hand was empty.

Mission accomplished. I turned my attention to the menu. "Since this was your choice, what do you suggest?" I asked.

We kept the conversation light as we conversed between bites of potato salad and hot pastrami sandwiches. He regaled me with the horrors of a hospital stay—the humiliation of being bathed daily by a candy striper, the blood pressure cuff expanding and squeezing his arm at regular intervals waking him up during the night, having a thermometer thrust under his tongue at inopportune times, a doctor penetrating his eyeballs with a pin light several times a day, and the disgusting bill-o-fare they called food.

I was really feeling sorry for him but much relieved when he finally smiled and said, "You should see the look on your face, Cooper. Had ya going there for a minute, didn't I? All joking aside, I thank God for our medical personnel. I couldn't have asked for any better treatment. Look at me!" he said and spread his arms wide, "I'm as good as new."

Thornton played his role beautifully — even though he may or may not have known he was role playing. If hostiles were lurking, I didn't spot any, and if there were, they wouldn't have detected anything unusual as everything went according to Hoyle.

• • •

After lunch, on our way out to the parking lot, I said, "Take care, my friend. The item I passed you is a hot commodity."

"I think I know what it is," Thornton said under his breath. "And I'll exercise due diligence."

"I know you will. In retrospect," I continued, "I suspect Doyle was not the only mole in the department. It seems the opposition is always a jump ahead of us. It was pure luck, if you can call it that, that Kenny went over the balcony before he could kill all of us. And even though Doyle was on a different continent, Lexington had the resources to have him on the scene in Cairo the very next day picking up where Kenny left off. Much too organized and convenient for a *mom-and-pop operation*."

Thornton nodded. "Nothing surprises me anymore. The mastermind behind this fiasco keeps moving people around like pawns on a chess board. Lexington had a lot of money pumped into his campaign, so someone out there took a gamble and put a lot of dough on the line and it appears is now calling in the chits."

"Any idea who that someone might be?" I asked.

Thornton looked thoughtful for a few moments. He finally said, "Hmm, maybe. My sister's middle daughter, Tanya, is a high school junior this year and a pretty sharp cookie. She was one of those selected to serve as one of the Senate pages from Colorado. She's so excited about being in *the heart of the government* she's on the phone every evening with my sister relating her experiences as a Senate page. The pages serve as messengers and attend to the diverse needs of the senators. Their duties include delivering correspondence and legislative items in and around the Senate complex. They're also charged with delivering bills and amendments to the chairperson's desk. Sis says Tanya is grateful to have the opportunity to be part of government, even on such a small scale, and being in the Senate Chamber makes her feel very important. Her duties keep her close to our elected officials all the time she's on the Senate floor, and she, of course, pays strict attention to Colorado's two senators who are credited for her appointment.

"My sister said that, during their conversation one evening, Tanya told her that she overheard several of the senior senators talking about Senator Lexington. She said they expressed surprise that, since Lexington was a first-term senator, he was lobbying for a position on the Foreign Relations Committee as well as the Subcommittee on Trade. Sis said Tanya told her that foreign relations and trade were sensitive areas and most of the committee and subcommittee members were at least second or third term senators. Tanya said the senators she overheard remarked that Lexington fell just short of demanding he be appointed to both the committee and subcommittee."

"Very interesting," I mused. "And was he?"

"Sis said Tanya verified that the president of the Senate, our country's vice-president, did appoint him to the Foreign Relations Committee as well as the Subcommittee on Trade, albeit under protest by some of the other members seeking those positions and who were obviously more qualified than Lexington."

"That's all very interesting," I responded. "Wonder if those appointments were sweetened with a favor."

"From what we've learned so far and knowing how politics work, your guess is as good as mine," Thornton replied with a smirk. "*One good turn deserves another*—especially among the legislative elite. They scratch each other's back like they had fleas!"

"And my guess is that it sounds like our friend is in bed with the Sabenese," I said, and we all know they have plenty of money to throw around. Don't believe anyone would contribute millions to an unknown's campaign without a pretty sure *quid pro quo* lurking in the wings."

"And you don't have to be an Einstein to figure out the payoff probably entails a Sabenia oil deal," Thornton stated. "Why else would Lexington be so insistent he be appointed to those specific committees."

After a pause, Thornton continued, "Thanks to my smart niece, Tanya, I also learned anyone can access the officially published House and Senate hearings online. They're available on the *govinfo* website. It might be interesting to see what kind of *most-favored-nation status* Lexington proposes to extend to the Sabenese in exporting their oil to America. I wouldn't be a bit surprised if Lexington favors minimizing or maybe even eliminating altogether quotas and tariffs on every barrel of oil imported to our shores from Sabenia. In other words, no import controls and *carte blanche* licensure."

"Bingo!"

···

Lexington was emboldened thinking he was now in possession of the incriminating evidence and there was nothing to link him to Margot's murder. He went into the Senate hearings with renewed gusto. He knew he had to bully the committee into voting in favor of the Sabenese oil deal that he made with Sahib Abakali in exchange for the cash he needed to get elected. From his past habits of forcing his will on others, he most likely felt bullying the committees would be a piece of cake.

As soon as Lexington put forward his proposal that the United States purchase the Sabenese oil glut, without the usual controls, the fight was on!

Four-term Texas Senator Theo Calhoun had the floor. Senator Calhoun was not timid about speaking his mind, and after serving four terms, he frequently did so. He stood and boldly laid it on the line. "Your proposal, Senator Lexington, defies all logic. It would be ludicrous to buy oil from a foreign nation when we ourselves have a glut that we can tap into for a fraction of the cost you're proposing. Also, why the elimination of import controls when such an act is not only unusual but unwarranted. I ask you, sir, why would we pay to transport oil all the way from Sabenia when we have plenty here in our own country? Have you already lost sight that you're working for the Americans, not the Sabenese?" he demanded. It was obvious Calhoun was barely in control of his temper, apparently incensed by what he described as Lexington's insane proposal.

Although he would've liked to have ripped Calhoun's heart out on the spot, Lexington promised himself he'd keep his temper in check. Wouldn't do for the other members of the committee to have to decide how to vote between two madmen. "Like I previously stated," Lexington countered in an authoritative voice, "after the last administration's disastrous foreign policies resulted in complete failure, we must do everything in our power to rebuild our relationships with foreign governments. And one way we can show our sincerity is by purchasing the oil glut from the Sabenese. By not requiring tariffs or import taxes, which would only be passed onto the American consumer, we can hold down the price per barrel significantly!"

"To hell with that!" Calhoun snorted. "Let the ragheads peddle their glut elsewhere. We Americans don't need, what you call, a relationship with the Sabenese. Sabenia is not an impoverished nation, sir! Since when does their Shambu need more money? Our sworn duty is to the citizens of the United States of America, not Sabenia or any other foreign entity for that matter. Our constituents expect us, and rightfully so, to enrich our own country first! What in bloody hell is it going to take for you to realize that?"

"Here, here!" came the reply from several other senators in attendance.

Lexington blanched. He was not accustomed to being called down, especially before a Senate committee. And after several other committee members agreed with Calhoun, Lexington's confidence was rapidly dwindling. He apparently thought his proposal would be welcomed with open arms and readily accepted by the committee. It was not. *My God! What if I can't deliver?* Shoving his clammy hands into his pockets, Lexington remembered only too well the swipe salute of his co-conspirators and their method of enforcing contracts. And it wasn't a long-drawn out court action for breach of contract or more aptly specific performance!

Chapter Eleven

Seeing is Believing

"Jack! This video is dynamite!" Thornton blurted into my ear as soon as I answered the phone. "There's no doubt it was Lexington who pulled the trigger."

"I thought so, too, particularly after viewing it on a larger monitor. The cellphone version was pretty weak, and I couldn't be sure." I paused before asking, "Now with confirmation and compelling evidence, what's your plan of action?"

"I wanted to discuss that with you," Thornton replied. "As far as I know, our little secret is still a secret and I'm sure Lexington will stay right where he is, so we don't need to worry about him fleeing to avoid prosecution.

"I've developed a severe case of paranoia, after all the recent events, regarding who I can trust and who I can't. Why, I would've laid down my life for Doyle. It's occurred to me that, quite obviously, I'm not such a great judge of character. Now, I second-guess all my decisions and find myself mistrusting almost everyone until they prove differently—and even then, I'm skeptical."

"Believe me, I know the feeling. However, the bottom line is that it's essential that we get the video to the DA in order to get an arrest warrant in the works," I said. "Do you think we can trust Henderson?"

"I've always had a good rapport with him professionally. As politicians go, Henderson seems to be a fair-minded district attorney. However, I don't know much about his personal life." Long moments lapsed before Thornton finally asked, "Will you go with me to meet with him? A united front may influence his decision to seek a warrant for Lexington's arrest. Plus, you may be needed as a witness or an affiant."

Without hesitation, I answered, "Yes! Schedule an appointment, and I'll be there!"

• • •

Thornton set up an appointment asking the DA's secretary for time "at the DA's earliest convenience." Because of Thornton's status as chief of detectives, the DA's secretary didn't ask for details regarding the appointment. However, she must've assumed it was an important matter because of the apparent urgency and scheduled us for that very afternoon.

When we were escorted into the DA's private office, Henderson extended his hand first to Thornton. "Russ, good to see you up and around.

We were all worried about you. How've you been doing?"

"Not too bad. I have an occasional headache but otherwise I seem to be recuperating from the concussion." Then pointing to me, Thornton stated, "You of course know Jack Cooper."

"Indeed, I do," Henderson replied, and we shook hands. "Come in and grab a seat." Once we were situated around Henderson's desk, he asked, "Now, what's this all about?"

"I have something I want you to see," Thornton said in a hushed voice. "I must first warn you, you're in for a shock."

"That so? Donno, after almost eight years as a DA prosecuting every kind of crime there is, I'd be a hard one to shock," Henderson said with a grin.

Thornton grinned back and produced the thumb drive. As he pushed it across Henderson's desk with his forefinger, he said, "I'd make you a wager on that, but don't want to take your money."

Henderson looked at Thornton and then me. If he was skeptical, it didn't show. "Okay," he responded. "You have my attention." Picking up the thumb drive he inserted it into his CPU. Thornton and I sat in silence as the DA viewed the video.

At the conclusion of the viewing, Henderson reared back in his chair, and still looking at his computer monitor, asked, "Where'd you get this video?"

Thornton and I took turns relating the entire sordid story, bringing the DA up to speed. Henderson looked at Thornton with a stunned expression when Thornton told him of Doyle's deceit.

"Glad I didn't make that wager," Henderson said. "I am, just as you predicted, totally shocked!"

When I related our trek across the pyramids with Doyle in hot pursuit, Henderson shook his head, apparently in disbelief. "Sounds like a scene from an *Indiana Jones* movie," he said.

"Believe me," I continued, "crawling across the hot pyramid felt like something out of a horror movie. We found out later that Doyle, after being left by his guide at the pyramids, was nearly dead when a camel driver picked him up and transported him to Cairo on one of his camels. It's an eight-mile hike from the pyramids back to Cairo, and the desert is unforgiving. If not for the camel driver, Doyle would surely have died."

"Most likely. I cringe just thinking about it. What happened after he was rescued?" Henderson asked.

Thornton picked up where I left off. "We understand he was in the hospital when he called and turned his resignation in to the police department.

We were all perplexed since no one had an inkling he was so disenchanted with his job," Thornton commented. "Even though it's unlikely attempted murder charges would stick since the crime was committed in Egypt, it appeared Doyle didn't want to take any chances and had had enough. Call it remorse or fear or a healthy dose of both, especially after learning Jack was onto him and his affiliation with Lexington as a gun for hire." Thornton then shook his head, apparently thinking of Doyle's deceit. "It's pretty obvious why he just wanted to disappear. I would, too, if I had all that baggage to contend with."

Through the rest of our narration, Henderson sat and listened with only an occasional interruption when he needed clarification. At the end of our dissertation, he said, "This is pretty powerful stuff. However, before I put my ass on the line and go to a judge to obtain an arrest warrant for a United States senator, no less, I'll need verification ensuring the tape wasn't *doctored*."

"That's fair," Thornton replied. "And I wouldn't expect a judge to issue an arrest warrant without verification that the evidence was legitimate, even if it wasn't for a U.S. senator. I'm making this top priority," Thornton promised. "I'll call you as soon as it's confirmed."

As we were rising to leave, something occurred to me and I called out, "Wait!"

Looking surprised, Thornton stopped midstride on his way to the door and glared at me.

Henderson frowned. "Yes?" he quired.

"Detective Thornton and I have been having issues with leaks, and not just restricted to the police department. Not only did Doyle turn out to be a mole, but now that we have evidence that a sitting U.S. senator committed cold-blooded murder and dispatched two of his paid assassins to take care of the potential witnesses, how can we be sure there aren't more moles in the department and that someone in the police lab or otherwise isn't on the take? If we turn the evidence over to the police lab for example and there's another mole, the video may just mysteriously disappear. Also, our target will then be forewarned and cover his tracks before we can do anything about it."

Thornton nodded. "Good thinking, Jack," he said and looked to Henderson, apparently expecting the DA's take.

"I agree that that's a valid concern," Henderson said emphatically. "However, I'm not sure with what's at stake how we can trust just anyone to confirm the integrity of the tape."

We all stood in silence pondering the problem.

Finally, Henderson said, "One of our former DA investigators, Gordon Blackstone, retired a couple of years ago. He was, and is, a crack photographer and develops his own work. He did a lot of work for the department and was good enough at his trade to start his own photography business when he retired. I hear he's going great guns. With your approval, I could ask Gordy to examine the tape. He's skilled enough to recognize if it's been tampered with and professional enough to keep his examination under wraps if requested to do so." Henderson continued, "Additionally, Gordy has the credentials to be certified as an expert witness should he be needed to testify at the hearings and of course the trial."

I looked at Thornton. He raised his brow. I nodded.

Thornton then asked Henderson, "How do you want to work the chain of custody?"

"Good question. I suggest you personally take the thumb drive to Gordy. Let him know it's evidence, and with his law enforcement experience, he'll know how to properly handle it since *everyone* through whose hands the evidence passes will be required to testify. Any break in the chain, of course, will make the proffered evidence inadmissible. It will be as if it never existed," Henderson said. "Take a blank receipt with you and have Gordy sign it verifying that he received the evidence from you on this date. Also, you need to go back and develop the chain of custody from the time you took possession of the tape. Make sure all who handle the evidence date and initial a receipt. You can bet Lexington will get the best defense attorney money can buy when and if he's arrested. With what's at stake here, we need to *play it by the book*."

・・・

When we left the DA's office, we went straight to Gordy's photography studio. The painted wooden shingle that hung over the entrance read *Flash Gordon's*. Very clever, I instantly knew I was gonna like Gordy.

"Hey, Russ," Gordy, who was standing behind the counter, greeted Thornton as we entered. "Henderson phoned and said you were on your way with a special project."

"Long time no see!" Thornton said as he looked around the interior of the shop. "This is quite the layout." Then looking at me and pointing, he announced, "This here's Jack Cooper."

"Pleasure," Gordy said. "Your reputation proceeds you!"

"I know better than to ask this," I said as we shook hands, "but was what you heard good or bad?"

"Depends! If you're on the right side of justice,

good. Otherwise…" Gordy responded with a broad smile.

"Enough with the back-patting," Thornton said and passed a clear plastic bag containing the thumb drive to Gordy along with a blank receipt.

As Gordy filled out the receipt, he asked, "Henderson said this project was strictly confidential. What's with all this cloak and dagger mystic?"

"I guess you could call it eyewitness evidence to a murder, or more aptly a reflection of a killer," Thornton replied.

Gordy softly whistled.

Thornton continued, "Did Henderson also advise you that until an arrest was made, this is to be kept under wraps?"

"Indeed, he did," Gordy said and handed the signed receipt back to Thornton saying, *"Loose lips sink ships."*

Pocketing the receipt, Thornton asked, "How long do you think it'll take to examine the film?"

"Not more than a day or two at the most. Henderson told me this job was top priority, so I'll start the minute you leave."

"Great!" Thornton exclaimed. "I'm a phone call away."

• • •

The next afternoon I received a call from

Thornton. "There's absolutely no evidence of tampering," he related. "I just hung up with Gordy and he's positive the video evidence is in its original form."

"That's great news!" I responded. "I would've bet a month's pay that the video was legit. Paige was totally devoted to her sister, and I know she wouldn't doctor the evidence which, if any tampering was discovered, would give Lexington an opportunity to get away with murder."

"Since basically the video is the only evidence we have, we need to ensure its integrity and safety. I'm on my way to pick it up from Gordy. Wanna ride with me?"

"Sure," I said. "A pair of extra eyes is a good idea. And I've been packing *Ole Faithful* since all the attempts to get rid of me. What's the use of having a gun if you can't use it?"

"Well, I had my weapon on me when I was knocked on the head, so there's no guarantee it's a guardian angel." After a brief pause, he added, "Meet me in front of your place in ten minutes."

• • •

Gordy was waiting for us behind the counter when we entered his shop. "This one's on the house," he said, as he handed the plastic bag containing the video back to Thornton. "The payback will be when you convict that rat bastard."

"Thanks, pal. We may need you to testify when and if the case goes to trial," said Thornton.

"Ready, willing, and able!" Gordy responded. "I've seen some pretty graphic stuff in my time but to casually walk up to your wife and shoot her was…was as cold blooded as it gets."

• • •

Back in the car, Thornton smiled and said, "Chief gave me the green light to present a warrant request to a judge if Gordy verified that the tape hadn't been tampered with. Just in case, I prepared the affidavit while I waited for Gordy to complete the examination. You see, I, too, had faith that the video was what it purported to be. I even lined up a judge before picking you up."

"Good grief, man! What's come over you?" I smirked.

"Knock it off!" Thornton snarled. "My worth has been a long-established fact!"

• • •

Judge Rosenberger met us at his office door and beckoned us into his chambers when Tess, his clerk, announced we had arrived. "Come in, gentlemen," he barked. "Grab a seat and tell me what this fuss is all about! My tee time isn't until late afternoon."

Don't want the quest for justice to interfere with

your personal life! I wanted to say but didn't. *After all, as Shakespeare pointed out, the better part of valor is discretion!*

The judge's face went through a myriad of expressions and colors as Thornton explained the circumstances.

At the conclusion of Thornton's rendition and after reading the affidavit in support of the arrest warrant, the judge shook his head, "I don't believe it! I just don't believe it! Leonard Lexington, our newly-elected United States senator?" Sagging in his chair, Judge Rosenberger held out his hand. "Give me that warrant," he ordered. "And you're sure the facts check out?" he asked as he poised his pen above the signature line.

"Yes, sir. I wouldn't have requested a warrant if I weren't sure," Thornton replied.

"God help us all," the judge murmured as he signed the warrant. Then with a final flourish of the pen, he handed the fully executed warrant to Thornton and said, "Here you are, detective, signed, sealed, and delivered. And I assume you want this kept quiet until you execute the warrant."

"Yes, sir," Thornton answered and then added, "for obvious reasons."

The judge reared back in his chair, and still holding the pen, opined, "Breaking the law is never to be tolerated, especially at the government level where the laws are made and voters have placed their trust in their elected officials." It was obvious from his words and the tone of his voice that he was offended that one of our nation's esteemed law makers would commit such a heinous act especially on his own wife. Tossing the pen onto his desk in a show of disgust, he murmured, "When this gets out, there may be an uprising in the party and maybe even in the ranks of Congress."

"Most likely," Thornton replied, and very wisely left it at that since it was a known fact that the judge and the senator were members of the same political party.

• • •

On the way out of the judge's chambers, Tess stopped us. Nodding toward the judge's office, and with a hint of pride in her voice, said, "Our judge is rubbing elbows with the celebs."

Thornton looked at me and raised his brow. "What do you mean?" he asked.

"Well," Tess responded, "being a party member and large supporter of Senator Lexington, the judge has been invited to a post-victory celebration at the Denver Convention Center this coming Saturday." Tess glanced at Rosenberger's closed door as she continued, "It's probably not a well-kept secret so I'm going to say it. Judge told me Senator Lexington was on the party's short list for the next presidential nomination. And who knows, if the senator is elected, our judge may be on track to a Federal Court appointment and maybe even the United States Supreme Court."

Thornton looked at me again and I thought I saw concern written on his face. It was apparent that something was percolating in his head, so I remained stoic.

Tess continued: "I probably shouldn't have said anything since the celebration wasn't widely advertised and only a select few have been invited. Judge Rosenberger told me that Senator Lexington is scheduled to make an appearance at the convention center sometime during the festivities."

"You don't say," Thornton remarked and then he looked back toward the judge's closed door. The expression on Thornton's face changed to a broad smile or maybe it was a smirk.

"Yes, and it's apparently a big deal," Tess said and the pride in her voice was vivid. "Judge has been looking forward to attending ever since he received the invitation a week ago," she added.

The look on her face was pure delight and I felt sorry for her. *She's probably anticipating a position as an aid to the newest justice on the highest court*

in the land, I thought. Too bad for those who put
their trust in the likes of Lexington. His downfall is
going to disappoint and even hurt a lot of people.

"Thanks, Tess," Thornton said still sporting a broad smile.

I was perplexed at Thornton's apparent excitement at hearing about the post-election celebration. When we were in the elevator, I said, "You look like the cat that swallowed the canary! What was that all about?"

"My friend, thank your lucky stars. We just had a plum dropped into our laps," Thornton remarked. "A nice, big, fat, juicy one!"

Still confused by Thornton's excitement, I asked, "How's that?"

"Since Lexington now resides in D.C., our state must have jurisdiction over his person. Even if we arrest him there, we'll have to jump through a myriad of hoops to get him extradited back to Colorado to stand trial. It's the way the law works and that could take months, even years. However, if we arrest him in Colorado, our state has jurisdiction over him. Tess just unwittingly told us when and where in Colorado we could serve the warrant on the errant senator."

I smiled at Thornton. "You sly ole fox! I want to be there when you make the arrest."

"You deserve to be in on the action, and I'll see what I can do," Thornton promised as he strutted away apparently visualizing the moment Lexington's house of cards would be tumbling down.

Chapter Twelve

Time to Pay the Piper

Senator Lexington traversed the Senate corridors pressing through the ever-present horde of media. He was suddenly very popular with the press because the current hot topic was his dispute with Texas Senator Theo Calhoun over conflicting views regarding the U.S. purchasing Sabenese oil. Lexington didn't have a personal bodyguard assigned to him. Only congressmen in *leadership* positions have personal bodyguards. Others do not unless they pay for them personally. The U.S. Capitol Police assume the safety of everyone in the Capitol building, so Lexington had to fend for himself if there were no officers in the vicinity to keep the press at bay. The reporters constantly jammed mics in his face bombarding him with questions to which he would ordinarily bark, "Get the hell outta my way," as he shoved his way through the crush as he headed for his office.

Lately, it seemed Lexington was always angry about something and was easily annoyed. However, this afternoon his mood appeared to be even more foul as he roughly plowed through the TV crews, forcing them aside with his forearm resembling that of an NFL running back trying to score a touchdown.

Taking long strides, he proceeded toward the sanctity of his office. "…and who does that hick from Texas think he's dealing with?" Lexington was shouting as he burst through his office door. One of his aides, Andy Taggert, trailed along behind the senator absorbing the brunt of his rage. "How dare that two-bit clown try to strongarm the committee into rejecting my proposal!" Lexington's face was crimson, dark circles underscored his eyes, and deep lines marched across his once smooth forehead and cheeks. It was obvious, even to an amateur that the senator's stress level was completely off the charts. His staff knew to lay low when he was in the midst of one of his mood swings.

"Excuse me, senator," Rosalee, his congressional secretary, said in a timid voice. When he turned, she stood and handed him something.

"What the hell is this?" Lexington snorted as he grabbed the envelope from her.

"Your plane tickets, sir."

"Oh, ah, of course. Thank you, Rosalee. I'd forgotten for a moment that this was my weekend to travel to Colorado," Lexington said. "Wouldn't want to disappoint my fans in Colorado now would I?"

"No, sir. And here are your calls," Rosalee said handing him a stack of pink telephone messages.

Lexington glanced at the stack. The top message was from Ammon. He then hurried into his office and slammed the door behind him. Seated at his desk, Lexington rubbed his eyes and groaned, thinking, *Since they retrieved the video for me, they're becoming even more relentless. That damned Calhoun...* Not having any good news to report to the Sabenese, he chose not to return the call to Ammon. He flopped his head against the cushioned back of his chair and stared at the ceiling. *Maybe the trip to Denver will revive me.*

• • •

Thornton phoned me the day after we received the signed warrant, "Jack, I'll need backup when I make the arrest but not sure I can trust anyone on the force not to alert Lexington before we can execute the warrant. Since you expressed some interest in being in on the action, I can commission you to assist me. Law enforcement can invoke what's called the *Posse Comitatus* Act to engage the help of citizens to aid police officers. As of now, you're official!"

"A posse? Hell, yes!" I blurted. "Just like the old west! I'll saddle up Ole Paint and together we'll cover your six."

"Ah, you're insufferable—"

"Hey, partner! Just having some fun, so lighten up would ya? Since Lexington was behind the attempt on our lives in Cairo, I have a dog in this fight, too! Remember? Of course, I want to help do the *honors*. Do you know his ETA?"

"No, but that's irrelevant!" Thornton said emphatically. "We do know he's scheduled to make a speech at Saturday's gathering at the Convention Center thanking his supporters for their generous contributions to his election and spurring them on in his quest for the presideny. I think we should take him down there in front of all his rich cronies—including Judge Rosenberger unless, of course, the judge decides not to show up."

"I've been giving that some thought. You don't think Rosenberger would tip him off, do you?" I asked.

"No, I don't. I think the judge is an honest man. He just bet on the wrong horse and doesn't want to be present when his plug comes in last."

"Right!" I said and quickly added, "Not to mention saying goodbye to any judicial appointment aspirations—at least not in the near future and maybe never."

• • •

Saturday evening, Thornton and I stood at

the entrance of the convention center looking for Lexington. I was not surprised when I didn't see Judge Rosenberger in attendance. The rich contributors and supporters were seated at round tables covered with white linen cloths and decorated with red, white, and blue carnation centerpieces. *Very patriotic,* I thought as I scanned the crowd. *If only they knew what was coming!* Dinner was being served by the waitstaff. The clatter of silverware against china, the clinking of crystal glasses, and the buzz of conversation filled the venue.

Still not seeing the senator, I looked over and noticed Thornton appeared to be anxious, so I remarked, "Maybe he hasn't arrived yet. You know how celebs like to be *fashionably late*," I said.

Thornton frowned. "Fashionably late or just not coming at all," he remarked. "Maybe I misjudged Rosenberger." Disappointment was evident in Thornton's voice.

Before I could respond, the MC, who was seated along with several other elite attendees on the stage at the head table, stood and tapped his butterknife against his waterglass. "Ladies and gentlemen, our guest of honor has just arrived…"

"This is it." Thornton whispered. "Come on." With that, he grabbed my arm and guided me into the proscenium off-stage left. We made it just in time to watch Senator Lexington stride out onto the stage from the proscenium off-stage right. The attendees stood and clapped. Many shouted and cheered as Lexington made his much-anticipated appearance.

However, the applause subsided and was replaced by a low mummer when Thornton and I *indiscreetly* made our debut and moved toward Lexington who was standing center stage next to the MC. The MC turned toward us and blared into the mic, "What's the meaning of this?"

"I'm Detective Russel Thornton and this is Jack Cooper," Thornton announced in a loud voice. "We have a warrant for the arrest of Senator Lexington."

"What!" the MC snorted, then looking around, perhaps seeking the straight man, he added, "This must be some kind of practical joke."

"Sorry, pal, no joke," Thornton replied, and removing the arrest warrant from his jacket pocket, approached Lexington and handed it him. Lexington stood as if paralyzed and stared at us. When Thornton shoved the paperwork into Lexington's chest, Lexington finally accepted it, albeit he appeared to be in a trance. The attendees, apparently sensing something significant was in the offing became eerily silent.

Lexington finally looked at the warrant and

apparently seeing the words *Arrest Warrant*, at the top of the paperwork, his eyes widened, and he suddenly came out of his daze, demanding, "What! What's this all about?"

Removing cuffs from his beltloop, Thornton positioned Lexington's arms behind his back and snapped the cuffs into place around Lexington's wrists. "You're under arrest for the murder of your wife, Margot Lexington," Thornton said in a voice loud enough to be heard throughout the venue.

"Margot…" Lexington said but stopped midsentence.

Thornton continued, "You're hereby advised that you have the right to remain silent. Anything you say can and will be used against you in a court of law. You have the right to an attorney. If you cannot afford an attorney, one will be appointed for you." After a pause, Thornton asked, "Do you understand your rights as I have read them to you?"

The buzz of those in attendance bespoke of shock. No one sought to intervene. Not even members of Lexington's entourage or the event security interfered with the arrest. Since the Denver police had jurisdiction, it appeared all were too stunned to react.

"This can't be happening! Are you crazy! You can't prove that, and you can't do this!" Lexington blurted as he jerked his arms around wrestling with the cuffs.

"Oh, on the contrary, we *can* do this. See, it says so right there on this officially issued warrant," and Thornton shook open the warrant in one fell scoop and read the language that stated: "…that the defendant be brought before the nearest available magistrate or judge without delay… And senator, that's just exactly what we intend to do." Then taking Lexington by the arm, he forced him from the stage.

Still cuffed and now seated in the back seat of Thornton's cruiser, Lexington pelted us with a variety of obscenities as he was being transported to the Denver County jail. "…and you'll regret the day you were born by the time I get through with you!" he shouted when he wasn't calling us unsavory names and threatening us with lawsuits for false arrest and defaming his good name in public.

I looked over at Thornton. His smile stretched from ear-to-ear. "Anyone ever tell you that you have a mean streak," I asked.

"Best kept secret in town!" he smirked.

"Not anymore!" I replied as we both stiffed an ill-advised laugh."

• • •

The melodrama unfolding around the senator was too good to miss, so the next morning, I was present when Lexington appeared before Judge Bradington Rankin for a bond hearing. Lexington was brought into the courtroom clad in an orange jumpsuit. Even I had to admit, he looked pretty pitiful sitting at the defense table with a public defender. He apparently didn't have enough clout to get a modern-day Clarence Darrow on board before his bond hearing.

"Mr. Lexington," the judge began—

"Beg your pardon, Your Honor. You will address me by my proper title!" Lexington demanded in an authoritative voice. After all, he was a sitting United States senator!

Yeah, like this judge is going to cut him some slack for being a senator, I mused. *His position may well be used against him for betraying the people's trust.*

"I consider his position more of a sword than a shield," Thornton leaned over and whispered to me.

Judge Rankin wasted no time letting everyone present, especially the high and mighty Lexington, know the judge was in charge. "Mr. Lexington, in my courtroom everyone is equal. Your title carries no weight here!" the judge reprimanded.

Having the wind knocked out of his sails,

Lexington shrank back into his seat and looked like a whipped puppy. The judge continued, "Even though the charge against you is first degree murder, you're still entitled to bail. That is unless the district attorney can convince me that the proof of guilt is evident and or the presumption of guilt is great." Then looking at Henderson, His Honor raised his brow.

Henderson stood and emphatically stated, "Your Honor, unlike most other murder prosecutions, we have a video of the defendant committing the homicidal act—the *reflection* of the killer forever etched in granite, if you will!"

Lexington didn't remain subdued for very long. He was instantly on his feet, his face red with rage. "I protest!" he shouted so violently he spewed spittle. "That's a lie! If there is such a video, it's a fake since I did not kill my wife!" Lexington's public defender tried to get him to sit back down but to no avail. Lexington jerked his arm out of his attorney's hand and ranted on, loudly proclaiming his innocence. "In my senate positions on the Foreign Relations Committee and the Subcommittee on Trade, I seem to have alienated a lot of people. Apparently, someone has created a phony video in order to frame me and destroy my career."

Obviously, Judge Rankin was not impressed

with Lexington's outburst. "Please take your seat, Mr. Lexington," the judge ordered, peering over his glasses with fire in his eyes. He then removed his glasses, and pointing them in the direction of the district attorney, asked, "What say you, Mr. Henderson?"

"Your Honor, a picture is worth a thousand words. I have a duplicate of the video with me today. Would you like to view it?" Henderson asked and held up the incriminating piece of evidence.

"Be that as it may," the judge said. "Since, this is a bond hearing and we're not here to determine innocence or guilt and in light of Senator Lexington's assertion that the video is pure fabrication, I will allow bail and set the bond at one million dollars—cash, property or surety. A condition of bond is that the defendant is prohibited from leaving the jurisdiction of the court without a judge's permission."

I noticed a stunned look on Henderson's face apparently about the same time as did the judge. He, the judge, quickly added, "The court is not ruling at this time that the video is contrived, or photo shopped—only that its admissibility must be established by competent evidence at the time of its introduction, presumably at trial."

Relief was evident in Henderson's voice when

he responded, "Thank you, Your Honor."

• • •

Back in his cell, Lexington began wondering who he could get to post bail. He didn't have a million dollars, and he didn't have any friends or even acquaintances who had a million dollars, either liquid or in assets that would risk it to help *him* out. He flopped back on his cot and stared up at the ceiling. Then it hit him like a ton of bricks. *The Sabenese!* Lexington had Ammon's cellphone number memorized, and when he asked, one of the guards was kind enough to let him make the call.

The Sabenese had, of course, been following the newspaper accounts of Lexington's arrest. Apparently, the Sabenese were becoming impatient with the *senator* and Ammon was quick to cut to the chase when he answered his phone. "So, it appears you find yourself in a predicament even after the Sahib obtained the video for you. What is it you want from us now?"

"I need help in getting out of here if I'm going to prove my innocence."

"Ah-ha!" Ammon snorted. "Since they now have evidence of your guilt, how do you propose you're going to prove otherwise?"

"By claiming the video is a fake and photoshopped or tampered with, a good attorney would be able to convince a jury of reasonable doubt." Lexington pleaded.

"I see," Ammon said. Then after a pause, he added, "I must confer with the Sahib." He then disconnected.

Lexington sat staring at the dead phone for a few moments. At least, Lexington thought, *he didn't give me an outright no! That's positive.*

• • •

Upon learning of Lexington's situation, Sahib Abakali was visibly upset. "After all we've done for that infidel…" he snarled. "Shambu Oman is becoming restless with the delay in getting the oil glut sold. If I lose face with the Shambu over this debacle, the American courts won't have to hold a trial. Our friend will just vanish from the face of the earth—piece-by-piece."

Apparently, as a last-ditch effort, Abakali instructed Ammon to find out the details and post bail for Lexington. Now, seated on the visitor's side of the plexiglass partition that separated the visitors from the prisoners, Ammon conversed with Lexington by use of a telephone.

"Sahib Abakali wanted me to convey his displeasure at your arrest. We thought the problem was taken care of when we obtained the woman's cellphone."

"I know and I'm most apologetic. Please convey my apologies to the Sahib. Apparently, *the woman* made a copy, or even multiple copies of the video and one fell into the hands of law enforcement."

"I see," Ammon replied. "That being said, the Sahib asked me to find out what it is you expect us to do now."

Lexington glanced behind him, apparently to ensure no one was close enough to overhear their conversation. Obviously satisfied they were isolated, he said, "Believe me, I do not make this request lightly. I've got to get out of here, and I need someone to post a million-dollar bond."

"So, you're asking the Sahib to request that the Shambu put up another million dollars in addition to the millions already spent to ensure your election?" Ammon asked and raised his brow.

"Basically, yes. But just hear me out before you reject my proposal. As you well know, I am, or was, favored to be our party's presidential candidate two years from now," Lexington began.

"Yes, we know that and that was one of the deciding factors that spurred us to ensure your election to the Senate so as to help pave the way to the presidency," Ammon replied. "Now you're asking for more money. We're not sure the Shambu would want to do that since your previous promises have yet to be fulfilled."

"If I am elected president, I'm in sole control of my actions and I won't have to fight with narrowminded senators like that buffoon Calhoun. I decide whether or not the U.S. purchases oil from Sabenia."

"Isn't that placing a lot on future events? You now have this trial to contend with. What if you are found guilty? Or, for that matter, what if you win the trial and not the presidency? Then we're out another million dollars."

"Believe me, I *will* be acquitted. There are ways to convince jurors on which way to vote. And after being acquitted of murder, I can see using my acquittal in a positive way in my campaign for the presidency. America loves heroes and being vindicated of murdering my beloved wife puts me in the hero category. I would then be placed in the category of *victim*."

Ammon sat looking thoughtful for a few moments. He finally said, "You make a good argument, and I will relate your message to the Sahib."

Because the Sabenese were reluctant to pay the non-refundable ten percent premium to a bondsman, they opted to post the entire amount of the bond, $1,000,000, in cash.

The next morning Ammon entered the lobby of the courthouse. He was carrying a valise full of U.S. currency. Ammon sat the case on the counter and said to the clerk, "I'm here to post bail for Senator Lexington. Here's the million dollars required to do so," and he pushed the valise toward the clerk.

It was obvious by the look on the clerk's face that she didn't believe Ammon was toting around a million dollars in a valise and she eyed him suspiciously. However, when she opened the case, her eyes grew wide. Rows of thousand-dollar bills were neatly banded and stacked in the valise. When she finally found her voice, she stuttered, "I…I've got to get my supervisor."

"I'll wait," Ammon said and grinned at her displaying perfect white teeth.

I heard later that, when the news spread, the clerk's office was in utter chaos, and it took almost an hour to authenticate and count the bills. The paperwork issued by the clerk was then hand-delivered to the sheriff's office and later to the jail.

That same day Lexington was released.

• • •

Having been restricted to the jurisdiction, he was prevented from returning to D.C. Once released, he took a taxi to Hertz and rented a vehicle. Fortunately, the mansion he shared with Margot in

Denver had not sold and was still available to him. The realtor had engaged a housecleaning service to keep the home pristine while it was on the market. Lexington contacted the realtors and advised them he was moving back into the residence for an undetermined length of time and to suspend the selling effort until further notice.

· · ·

The first item on Lexington's agenda was to procure a good defense attorney. He knew several in the area. However, the one that stood out was Steven DeVore. Lexington placed the call.

"Good morning," the cheery-voiced receptionist greeted. "How may I direct your call?"

"May I speak to Mr. DeVore?"

"Who shall I tell him is calling?"

"An innocent person charged with first degree murder," Lexington said and hoped the receptionist wouldn't ask any more questions.

Moments passed until finally Lexington heard, "DeVore here. If this is some kind of joke, hang up now. If not, state your business!"

Lexington liked the direct approach and congratulated himself for having chosen wisely. "My name is Leonard Lexington, United States Senator Leonard Lexington. Does that resonate with you?"

"I'm only familiar with your dilemma from what I've read and heard in the media," DeVore replied. "Needless to say, I need to interview you and you need to interview me. If you would like to schedule an appointment, I will arrange my schedule to accommodate you."

• • •

After their initial meeting, and Lexington having posted a retainer of $100,000, the source of which was questionable, DeVore entered his appearance.

"Certainly doesn't look like a killer!" DeVore's bookkeeper told him as she processed the retainer.

"Can't judge a book by its cover!" DeVore replied and raised his brow. "Guilty or not, even a United States senator deserves proper representation," he said as he headed for the office of the firm's crack investigator, Carlos Macada.

Chapter Thirteen

Trial of the Decade

The crowd gathering outside the courthouse the first day of trial reminded me of the carnival-like atmosphere surrounding the hangings in the 1800s that I had read about. After all, it was not every day citizens got to see a United States Senator tried for a capital offense, especially not first-degree murder and especially not one involving the homicide of a senator's spouse.

Because of the number of people clamoring to gain entrance, the trial judge restricted entrance into the courtroom to members of the media and those summoned for jury duty. A sheriff's deputy was stationed at the double doors to make sure there weren't any gatecrashers.

Lexington sat at the defense table with DeVore and DeVore's assistant, Pamela Wethington and the firm's investigator, Carlos Macada. Other than recording the names of jurors and making sporadic notations, Lexington appeared to be distracted and not the least bit interested in their responses. In fact, he looked bored with the whole process. DeVore would occasionally confer with Lexington over some of the answers provided by the potential jurors. However, Lexington for the most part just shrugged in reply. It was obvious by the look on DeVore's face that he was puzzled over Lexington's lack of concern and carefree attitude and wondered why Lexington was intent on taking notes during the jury *vior dire*, and after the jury had been selected, surreptitiously taking photos of the jurors with his iPhone—a no-no if he got caught.

Unknown to DeVore, Lexington, by previous arrangement, was in cahoots with the Sabenese. They would target one of the jurors to be a holdout during deliberations. Depending on the disposition of the chosen one, the bait would be money, threats, or both. Lexington would slip the list and the photos he compiled to Ammon. Ammon would then conduct an extensive background check on selected jurors in order to determine which ones would be best suited for a bribe.

• • •

After a week of vetting potential jurors, twelve were finally approved by both sides and once they were sworn and seated, the trial was underway. The prosecution called police department personnel, medical personnel, lab technicians, Gordy Blackstone, and a plethora of the usual witnesses used to establish a *prima facie* case. The prosecution reserved Paige Fontaine and her much-awaited testimony as its last witness. It was anticipated her testimony would be the *coup de grâce*.

After establishing identity and relationship to the deceased, the DA proceeded:

"Ms. Fontaine, do you remember what you were doing on September 15, the evening your sister was murdered?"

"Yes. We, Margot and I, were talking on the phone. She was streaming different poses of her wearing her new sunglasses. She was always insecure about her fashion selections and as far back as I can remember, I was her sounding-board."

"Did anything unusual occur during that conversation with Margot?"

"Yes."

"Will you explain to the jury what happened?" Henderson asked as he looked at the jurors.

I was closely watching Paige. She sagged in the witness chair and stared straight ahead for a few moments, apparently organizing her thoughts. She seemed overwhelmed by the whole process and tentative.

Moments passed and the DA finally prompted Paige. "Ms. Fontaine," he said, "would you like for me to repeat the question?"

Paige looked up and shook her head in answer

to the DA's question. Gathering her thoughts, she began, "You see, Margot and I shared our personal lives. Because of her husband's controlling nature, it was hard for her to have close friends. Leonard wouldn't allow it. No girlfriend lunches, no shopping, no bridge parties, no any other thing involving socializing with *outsiders*—his word, not hers. I was Margot's link not only to the past, but to the present and the outside world."

Paige paused and pulled a tissue from her pocket and dabbed at her eyes. She declined the judge's offer to take a brief recess and then continued. "The night of the murder, Margot called wanting my opinion regarding her new sunglasses. Margot's eyes had always been extremely sensitive to bright light, and when she heard that the new colored lenses actually helped filter out the light, she decided to try them. As she clowned, posing for videoing selfies, I remember laughing because the lenses reflected everything in the room when she turned her head."

As if watching everything unfold in front of her, Paige continued, "All of a sudden, Margot stopped streaming video. I figured Leonard had come home and she wanted to end the call before he caught her. Yes, *caught* her in the act of committing the unforgivable sin of talking to her sister without his express permission."

Paige faltered and emitted a loud sob and put her hand to her mouth. The judge leaned over his bench and asked, "Ms. Fontaine, the offer for a brief recess is still open!"

Paige shook her head. "No, thank you, Your Honor, I can do this."

"Very well, continue," the judge said in a sympathetic tone.

Still dabbing at her eyes, Paige related, "Leonard phoned me late that night and advised me of Margot's death. When he said she'd been murdered, I refused to believe it. I remember being so distraught, I couldn't think and must've been in denial because I immediately replayed the last video I received from her. I guess I was hoping there was some mistake and that she really wasn't dead. Watching the rerun of the video was when I discovered the end of the tape, revealed in her sunglasses, Leonard approaching her with a gun in his hand. I heard a loud bang just before the call ended. That was probably the shot that killed Margot."

I watched Leonard when Paige accused him of pulling the trigger. He remained stoic. His attorney, however, was on his feet.

"Objection!" DeVore bellowed. "Calls for speculation and conjecture on the part of the witness. Move the witness' answer be stricken."

Judge Rankin peered over his glasses as he said, "If you assert that the video would be the best evidence and would speak for itself, I'd sustain your objection."

Without a place to hide, DeVore grudgingly responded, "The defense would include that as part of their objection."

"Very well then," said Judge Rankin and thereupon turned to Henderson and asked, "Do you intend to play the video for the jury? And if so, wouldn't this be a good place to do so?"

"Your Honor, we were just interrupted by Mr. DeVore before we properly laid a foundation for admissibility of the video," Henderson replied. "We request leave to lay that foundation before offering the video in evidence."

"So granted," said Judge Rankin. "Since no offer has been made of the video, the court overrules Mr. DeVore's objection on the ground that it is premature. Mr. Henderson, you may proceed!"

"Thank you, Your Honor," Henderson said and continued. "Ms. Fontaine, I hand you what has been marked as People's Exhibit A and ask if you can identify it?"

Paige took the video from Henderson and carefully examined the exhibit before responding. "Yes," she said, "I can identify it! First of all, it contains my initials and the date. It's an exact duplicate of the video I referred to in my previous testimony."

"How do you know it's an exact duplicate?" Henderson asked.

"I examined it and verified its authenticity before I placed my initials and date on the label," Paige replied.

"The prosecution offers People's Exhibit A in evidence and requests that it be played for the jury," said Henderson as he positioned himself in direct line of the video player.

On his feet once again, DeVore was livid as he shouted objections. The video was tantamount to actually watching the murder and DeVore pleaded it was prejudicial to his client.

The judge finally regained control of the courtroom. Looking sternly at DeVore, he said, "I'm assuming you had the opportunity to view the video as part of the prosecution's evidence. And I just asked you if you would assert that the video would be the best evidence and would speak for itself, and if so, I would sustain your objection."

DeVore grudgingly took his seat and shook his head. He must have wondered why Lexington wasn't more reactive. But then, he was unaware that Lexington had an insurance policy or more appropriately an *ace-in-the-hole.*

The video had its intended effect. "How often is a video of the actual murder presented to the jury?" Henderson's assistant asked in a hushed tone. "The sunglasses are the *reflection of a killer.*"

"I've prosecuted over a hundred murder cases as either a deputy or a DA but this is a first. I should donate half my salary for the month to charity since I didn't really earn it," Henderson whispered.

Chapter Fourteen

The Fix

During jury selection, Ammon traded his Egyptian-style clothing for an American business suit. He sat in the back of the courtroom taking notes. He had previously garnered as much information as he could using the names and dates of birth supplied to him by Lexington as the basis of his extensive search for a juror they could bribe.

During his jail visits, Ammon also learned from Lexington that one juror, in particular, a man by the name of Anderson Evans, most likely was the kind of person they were searching for. Evans gave his profession as foreman for an auto manufacturer. Ammon perceived Evans was most likely a take-charge kind of person who demanded results from those under his charge, and because of his husky build, was probably a bully since birth.

Lexington informed Ammon, that during *vior dire*, he learned that Evans' twelve-year-old daughter had been diagnosed with a defective heart valve and needed expensive surgery to correct it. Otherwise, her life expectancy was morbid. Lexington also informed Ammon that Evans had been laid off work for over a year because of the Covid pandemic and that his insurance had lapsed. Evans stated that, like himself, other parents were without funds to pay exorbitant medical procedures and hospitals like *St. Jude* were overflowing. He said his daughter was on the list at several of the charity hospitals, but he was skeptical she would be admitted in time to save her life. Ammon did the research. The cost of heart valve surgery ranged from $80,000 to $200,000 or more with an average being in the neighborhood of $150,000.

Just the kind of person we're looking for!

• • •

Ammon attended the trial daily and watched Evans very closely. What the Sabenese were planning amounted to a one-time deal. If Evans refused, they couldn't just go pick another juror and offer a bribe. If Evans blew the whistle, they in all likelihood were dead in the water. Ammon planned his approach with precision, determination, and confidence. Failure might jeopardize more than his job. Expectations brought with it repercussions.

• • •

Seated in his rental car outside of Evans' modest home, Ammon waited. When Evans pulled into his driveway, Ammon exited his vehicle and approached him.

"I'd like to talk to you," Ammon said, as Evans opened the driver's door of his vehicle.

Stunned by the suddenness of Ammon's appearance, Evans strained his neck trying to determine from whence the stranger came. "What do you want?" Evans asked still holding onto the inside driver's door handle.

"Can we sit inside your car?" Ammon politely asked. "I have a bad back and can't stand for very long."

The stranger looked prosperous and nonthreatening even though he had an aura of mystery about him. Curiosity trumped caution and Evans nodded and opened the passenger's side door and Ammon slid in.

"Now, what's this all about?" Evans demanded as the two sat face-to-face.

"I want to help you with your child's surgery," said Ammon.

"You…you want to do what?" Evans stammered.

"Quite simply, pay for your daughter's surgery. By the way, what's her name?"

"Regina. How did you know about her heart condition in the first place and why would you want to pay for her surgery?" Evans asked in an incredulous tone.

In the first place, how I know doesn't matter,

and in the second place, your benefactor requests a small favor in return."

"Un-huh! Here it comes. And what does *my benefactor* want from someone like me?"

"A *not guilty* verdict!"

Evans was quick to react. "Whoa! That's illegal and I wouldn't do it for all the money in the world! How dare you attempt to cash in on my daughter's medical condition by asking me to break the law. Why, I should report this incident to the authorities. Jury tampering I'm told is a serious crime!"

"That would be a very unwise move on your part," Ammon said. Although his voice was quiet, it carried an unmistakable veiled threat. He continued by saying, "What's worse, breaking the law or losing a child? You think about it, and I'll be in touch." Ammon then exited Evans' vehicle and went back to his own and drove off into the sunset.

• • •

That night, Evans laid awake reflecting on the conversation he had earlier with Ammon. He knew what Ammon meant. If he didn't agree to vote not guilty then Regina would not likely survive. *Then again...if they're willing to pay $150,000 to save Regina's life...how can I refuse.* The bottom line was for him to sacrifice his integrity in return for his daughter's life. It was a no-brainer. The next day when Evans spotted Ammon in the courtroom, he very discretely nodded. The fix was in.

• • •

At the conclusion of the presentation of evidence and final arguments, the jury was escorted to the jury room to deliberate, and as fate would have it, Evans was elected foreperson. When they took the first vote, the count was eight to four in favor of guilty. Evans had his work cut out for him. He put up a pretty decent argument:

"The prosecution would have you believe having the murder on video tape should be all the evidence you need to convict. However, I'm an amateur photographer and in today's world, photoshopping is the norm, not the exception. It's even possible to superimpose another's face to change identities of those being photographed or videoed. I realize an expert with impeccable credentials verified that the tape had not been altered or tampered with, but I can assure you the pros can alter any photographic material without leaving a trace.

"Now, I ask you, why would a senatorial candidate, after a landslide victory, murder his wife of many years—especially after the two made plans to move to the nation's capital? Doesn't make sense to me, does it to you? We heard witnesses testify that the Lexingtons appeared to be a happy couple.

It's common knowledge that Lexington was being groomed to run for president in the next presidential election. Do you think he'd risk it all by committing murder? The real question is: *What motive did the prosecution prove?* Remember, the prosecution has the burden of proof. Defendants don't have to prove anything—not even their innocence.

"And I think you'd agree, that faced with the sudden death of a dear loved one, as was the victim's sister, you might be inclined to do what she did. She claimed to have seen Lexington approach and shoot her sister. She admitted that she didn't like the defendant, and in her distressed state of mind, she may have thought it was him who pulled the trigger. It makes more sense that someone who looked like Lexington broke into the house and killed Mrs. Lexington or that the victim's sister, convinced that Lexington killed her sister, hired someone with special talents to superimpose Lexington's face on the video. Just saying! I'm not convinced one way or the other. The jury instructions say the tie should go to the defendant."

Those stumping for conviction also put up a decent argument:

"Mr. Evans, with all due respect, I think you're distorting the evidence," juror number seven began. "I have a sister two years younger than myself and we keep in close touch and share our lives with one another. I think it's common, especially for sisters, to share intimate information with each other. You're forgetting to mention Paige also stated Margot complained about being controlled. Margot confessed to Paige that she wasn't in a happy marriage. However, running for senate, I'm sure in front of friends, the Lexingtons put on a good show. I believed Paige when she said she was sure the shooter was Leonard Lexington. I also believe the experts who testified here under oath that the video had not been tampered with."

And so it went for several days. When the last vote was eleven for conviction and one for acquittal and the jury hopelessly deadlocked, the judge declared a mistrial. The holdout, of course, was Anderson Evans.

Chapter Fifteen

The Battle Rages

Recess or no recess, the Sabenese were growing uneasy with the hiatus. Lexington was soon replaced on the Senate Foreign Relations Committee and dropped from the Subcommittee on Trade. No longer a member of either committee or chairman of the SFRC, the power he now wielded could fit in a thimble. He was soon a *persona non grata* and shunned by his colleagues as well as his own staff and was avoided as though he had the plague. It was obvious the Sabenese now considered him a liability.

Sahib Abakali sat gazing out of his window at the embassy as Ammon stood nearby, waiting. Abakali finally said, "The only thing the *infidel* accomplished in the short time he was in office was to alienate the committee and subcommittee members against any possible oil deal with our country."

It was apparent the Sabenese considered the racehorse they bet on was now ready for the glue factory. Needless to say, they were not alone. It has always been said that a black mark on one member of Congress is a black mark on all! Not wanting to be in the spotlight and thus subject to having *their* records examined by their constituents, party members disassociated from Lexington and left him to deal with his woes. No desire for guilt by association there.

Unable to cope without being subsidized, Lexington soon found he could no longer afford the services of an attorney let alone the DeVores of the world. Indigent, Lexington was forced to petition the judge for court-appointed legal representation. He soon was represented by a public defender by the name of Herbert Melon. Melon's claim to fame was not passing the state bar exam until the fifth try.

When I heard about Lexington's court appointed attorney, I almost felt sorry for them—Lexington and his attorney. If Lexington had a chance, even a chance in hell, it was a slim one.

The retrial started with a flurry thanks to the massive media coverage. Sensationalism, especially at the government level, sold papers like popsicles in the dead of summer, and the press had a heyday. The courtroom was packed to capacity and the press corps was limited to a select few. The Honorable Reginald Pfiffer, a retired State Supreme Court Justice, presided.

There were few surprises as the evidence

presented mirrored that of the first trial. However, pursuant to an anonymous tip during the hiatus, Lexington's financial records were examined. The major deviation was evidence of a mysterious fund in Leonard Lexington's name containing the same amount of money, excluding interest, as Margot paid to the so-called extortionist. The deposits were made in increments of $5,000 which coincided with the dates of the payments of the blackmail, or as the authorities referred to it, *hush money*. Although the mystery account was in his name, Lexington claimed he knew nothing about the funds and that the account he later found out had been set up by an accountant who had since died. Parts of the cross-examination went something like this:

"Your wife had a separate bank account containing funds she received by way of an inheritance from her late grandmother. Is that correct?" Henderson asked without looking up from his notes.

"Yes," Lexington replied and shifted nervously in the witness chair.

"Your name was not on the account Margot's grandmother established, was it?"

"No, I didn't expect it to be. Grandmother Fontaine made it clear she didn't approve of me and never was in favor of our marriage."

"You and Margot had a prenuptial agreement that declared that your separate property would remain your separate property and that in the event of a divorce it would not be considered part of the marital estate. Is that also correct?"

"Yes," Lexington answered. "Her grandmother was the one who insisted on the prenup." It was obvious Lexington was uncomfortable with this line of questioning. He continued to shift about in the witness chair resembling a feline that was unable to find a comfortable position.

"Would it be fair to say that the only way you would have access to the funds in that account was if Margot voluntarily relinquished control?" Henderson asked and looked up from his notes.

"Yes!"

"Did you ever ask her if you could borrow some of the money to bolster campaign contributions?"

"Yes, I did on one occasion. She said the account was her *security blanket* in the event something happened to me and that she had promised her grandmother on her death bed that the money would not be used except in a dire emergency," Lexington replied.

"So, I take it you asked but she refused thus honoring her pledge to her grandmother. Correct?"

"Yes, she refused even though I promised to

repay her with interest once I was elected. However, she was stubborn especially when it came to parting with her inheritance. Her grandmother apparently still controlled her—even from the grave."

Henderson ignored Lexington's comment concerning the grandmother. Lexington obviously had issues with Margot's family members. Instead, Henderson asked, "Is that why you staged the phony *extortion* or as it's sometimes called *blackmail* scheme?"

Lexington flushed as he tried to find words to dispel what he considered to be a myth and a question he considered unworthy of a dignified response.

"I…I…I *did not*, I repeat did not extort or blackmail anyone much less my own wife. How dare you insinuate such a thing," he began and then stammered, "I'm not rich or poor but don't, and never will, need money I'm not entitled to and would never, under any circumstances, utilize criminal means to benefit myself or anyone else."

Raising his brow, Henderson asked, "Well, senator, don't you think accepting millions of dollars from Sabenia and then using your position on the Foreign Relations or Foreign Affairs Committee and the Senate Subcommittee on Trade to broker a United States oil purchase from the Sabenese is tantamount to *utilizing criminal means to benefit yourself?"*

Lexington almost came out of the witness chair as he sneered, "The millions you allude to were campaign contributions. How dare you attempt to characterize it as some kind of bribe?"

Melon was again on his feet. His objection that Henderson's questions assumed facts not in evidence were summarily overruled by Judge Pfiffer. "Senator, just answer the question!" the judge admonished as he leaned forward over his bench glaring at Lexington. "It is a witness' job to answer questions—not ask them!"

"Sorry, Judge, but for the prosecuting attorney to attempt to make a bribe out of campaign contributions is an unfair characterization and prejudices my case," Lexington said as he sank back into his chair.

Melon was back on his feet. "Judge, we move for a mistrial because of the unwarranted and improper insinuations made by the prosecution. The jury has been exposed to what is classified under the law as evidence of other salacious and unproven acts and assumptions wherein the prejudicial effect on the jury is forever etched in their minds."

"Care to respond?" Judge Pfiffer asked Henderson.

"Yes, thank you, Your Honor. This is proper cross-examination," Henderson replied. "To challenge the defendant's statement that he *would never utilize criminal means to benefit himself* opened the door and I'm now clothed with the latitude of exposing the false and misleading nature of his assertion."

"Well stated," said Judge Pfiffer. "The intended objection is hereby overruled, and the motion for a mistrial is hereby denied. The witness is instructed to answer the question."

Melon took his seat looking like a scolded puppy.

"Would you like for me to repeat the question?" asked Henderson.

"No!" Lexington retorted. "For the last time, I'm not on the take and never have been. I can't help who financially supports my campaign and who doesn't. I pushed for the trade with the Sabenese because it was in our country's best interest. I've thought that all along and I still think it's in the best interest of our country. Whether the Sabenese also benefits, is of no particular concern to me—nor should it be of yours."

"Time out," said Judge Pfiffer, apparently having his fill of Lexington using the witness stand as a platform to justify his actions as a senator.

"This would be a good time for a recess. The court would like to see counsel in chambers!"

• • •

During the break one of the members of the press corps was overheard saying to one of his confederates: "If I were Lexington's attorney, I'd be more concerned about defending the first-degree murder charge than the uncharged extortion claim."

In chambers and out of the presence of the jury, with only the Judge, his court reporter, Henderson and Melon present, Judge Pfiffer vented his frustration.

"Mr. Melon, you could avoid having to make a lot of frivolous objections and wasting everyone's time if you would caution your client to answer *only* the question asked and not pontificate. By opening the door, the court has no choice but to allow Mr. Henderson wide latitude in his cross-examination. If you think you're making a record for appeal, you're badly mistaken. All that your client is doing is sealing his own fate. The state doesn't need Mr. Henderson to do that!"

All that was left for Judge Pfiffer to do was to order Melon to wear a dunce hat and go sit in the corner.

It appeared Judge Pfiffer had taken all the wind out of Melon's sails. "I'll...I'll... speak with my client before the court reconvenes," was all Melon could manage to mutter.

• • •

"Earlier," said Henderson as he continued his cross-examination of Lexington, "you stated Margot was reluctant to part with her inheritance. I then asked if that was the reason you staged the phony extortion plot. Remember me asking you that question?"

"Yes."

"And your answer?"

It appeared Lexington was determined to stick to his guns by refusing to compromise or alter his course of conduct. "I neither knew nor know of such plot. The simple answer is *no*, I did not stage it."

"Were you aware of the bank account that was set up in your name to log in monthly deposits of five thousand dollars? Remember, you're testifying under oath!"

"As I said earlier that must of been established by my now deceased accountant unbeknownst to me. In fact, I didn't know about it until it was mentioned in court."

"Would you agree that you were the beneficiary of those deposits?"

"I thought the law didn't recognize a gift until it was acknowledged by the person to whom the gift was to be made," Lexington smirked.

"You call extorting hush money a gift?" Henderson asked.

"Whatever it's called, I didn't know about it. Besides, if I knew about the funds, then why didn't I withdraw some or all of the money?" Lexington shot back. "I could've used the money!"

"Would it be because you had painted yourself into a corner and by withdrawing any of the funds you would have exposed your ruse?"

Lexington emitted an audible sigh before answering. "How many times must I tell you, I was never aware of the account!" he stated emphatically.

"So, you're saying that you didn't know your wife was being blackmailed?" Henderson asked relentlessly.

"Yes! That's what I'm saying. If she was, I had no knowledge of it."

"Had your wife done something that precipitated the extortion attempt?"

Looking exasperated, Lexington replied, "The only thing I knew about was that she had been involved in a hit and run automobile accident that resulted in someone's death."

"Come now, senator, wasn't it *you* and not your wife who was driving at the time of the fatality?" Henderson asked.

"Absolutely not!" Lexington retorted and came halfway up from his chair. "I wasn't even in the car at the time. If my wife hadn't told me about it, I would never have known about the severity of the accident. I thought she had just been involved in a minor fender-bender."

"If that be true, then why did you ask your wife to take the blame?"

"Why wouldn't I, if she was the one who was driving at the time of the so-called fatality?"

"Why would Margot tell her sister that you were the driver and wanted her to take the blame so that you wouldn't risk the adverse publicity that could cost you the election?"

Apparently frustrated, Lexington rubbed his brow before answering. "That figures. I don't doubt that Margot blamed me for the accident just as Paige testified during the prosecution's case, but what my wife related to Paige, was false."

"You were irate when Margot disclosed to her sister that you were the driver of the vehicle that struck and killed an innocent bystander, isn't that correct, senator?"

"Hell, yes! You would be, too, if you were falsely accused of something you didn't do. Irate maybe because she lied but not irate enough to kill my own wife. I loved her too much to do that!"

"Come now, senator. You want us to believe Margot, your wife, came first. Yet, you heard witnesses in the prosecution's case testify that you told them your career came first and *come hell or high water*, you would become a United States senator and ultimately president of the United States."

"Are you asking me if I heard that?"

"Yes, and whether or not those witnesses who testified under oath were telling the truth?"

"No, they're lying. I never told them or anyone else anything even remotely close to the idea that I would sacrifice my wife or my marriage for a political career. Why would I sacrifice my wife when I didn't need to? After all, at the time of Margot's death, I had already become a United States senator. What possible motive would I have?"

"To silence her perhaps. Transparency and disclosure of sordid facts would put an end to any political career or ambition. After all, you still had your eyes focused on the highest office in the land."

The remainder of Henderson's cross-examination of Lexington was most effective and focused on Lexington's motive to kill Margot (mainly his distrust that she would spill the beans on his involvement in the hit-and-run and his attempt to shift the blame; his quest to be elected to public office at all costs; and his deal with the Sabenese), Lexington's manipulation of public perception, and his total disregard for legal and ethical conduct.

As Henderson closed his notebook and stepped away from the podium, he announced, "No further questions."

Chapter Sixteen

Finale

After Lexington testified, but before the defense presented all its evidence, Sahib Abakali instructed Ammon to contact the Shambu.

Moments later, Ammon advised Abakali that the Shambu was on the phone.

"Naeam, yes, of course, put him through." Abakali immediately answered when his phone buzzed, "Your Royal Highness, I've been awaiting your instructions concerning *our friend*."

Shambu Oman dispensed with the usual formalities and cut to the chase. "After our previous conversation, I've given careful consideration to the situation," he said. "*Our friend* has become more of a liability than an asset. He's lost face with his colleagues. Having been ejected from the committee and the subcommittee, I doubt in his current circumstance he has enough clout to get our deal even up for consideration, much less accepted. In fact, he had been on the Senate Foreign Relations Committee as well as the Subcommittee on Trade for over six months and made no perceivable progress whatsoever. It appears his constant wrangling with his adversary, Senator Calhoun, has placed him in a bad light with his colleagues and he has lost ground not gained it."

Abakali knew better than to interrupt the Shambu, so he sat and listened, as the Shambu continued:

"We *donated* a king's ransom to Senator Lexington's campaign, not counting the million we posted in bail, and to date have received absolutely nothing in return except more excuses and being pulled into his personal crisis. The Americans have an old saying that refers to throwing *good money after bad.* I think we've reached that point. You know him better than I. What do you think his chances are of being acquitted and his reputation and influence restored?"

"Your Royal Highness," Abakali began, "I agree with your assessment. Even Lexington's argument that Americans worship heroes and that by being acquitted of murdering his wife would make him a hero doesn't fly in the face of reason. There will be a large number of the electorate who will disagree with an acquittal, and if the elected desire to stay in office, they listen to their constituents. And in my opinion, Lexington has underestimated the opposition and handled our deal poorly thus making it impossible for anyone else to resurrect the proposal. He has indeed become a liability." After a pause, he added, "He has become irredeemable!"

"It appears we're on the same page," the Shambu said. "We can't afford any loose ends that would taint or destroy our credibility with the Americans." He then added, "You know what to do—make sure it sends a message that we're not to be toyed with!"

"Yes, And I will follow your instructions to the letter, Your Highness."

• • •

Outside the metal detector at DIA, I paced the floor as I waited for Paige. Every so often I'd stop and scan the arrivals rushing toward the exit hoping I'd see Paige among them. It seemed to me that she'd been gone for months when in reality it was only a few days. My consolation was that she'd call me every night and assure me she was safe. However, I still fretted knowing she was back in Cairo where this fiasco began.

"Hey, stranger!" I heard someone say from behind me and I whipped around. Paige was standing there with a big smile and a twinkle in her eyes. I pulled her in an embrace, and she dropped her flight bag and wrapped her arms around my neck.

"I've been scrutinizing the arrivals watching

for you. How'd you manage to sneak up on me?" I asked as I gazed into her lovely face.

"Came out with the flight crew over there," and she pointed to a doorway behind the ticket counter.

Our welcome home ritual lasted only for a brief but cherished moment. We were both eager to leave the airport and go someplace where we could talk.

After clearing the traffic exiting the airport, I looked at my watch. It was 2:30 in the afternoon, and we were approaching the *IHOP* restaurant turnoff. I knew she probably hadn't eaten during the twelve-hour journey back to the states, so I said, "If you're hungry—"

She cut me off as she exclaimed, "I'm starved!"

"I take that as a *yes* — and no sooner said than done," I promised and took the offramp.

• • •

Once we were seated, I watched her examine the menu and realized how much I missed her. She wore her long brunette hair wrapped in a bun under the hijab when she was working. However, when we reached the car after I picked her up at the airport, she pulled her hair loose, and it now hung in soft waves over her shoulders framing her angelic face. Her big blue eyes complimented her *peaches and cream* complexion, and her full rosy lips completed the picture. "I missed you!" I said.

She looked up from the menu momentarily and said, "Missed you, too!"

"Will you marry me?" I asked and even surprised myself as that was the first I knew I was going to propose. It just came out.

Looking up from her menu, Paige replied, "Yes, I will marry you. But first if I don't get something to eat, I may not live long enough to do so."

"Very romantic," I teased. "I often wondered how I'd propose to the girl of my dreams but over coffee at an *IHOP* was never one of the scenarios."

"Look at it this way," Paige said with a wide grin, "it'll be good for a laugh when we're old and gray and exchanging love stories with our friends at the assisted living facility."

After placing our order, Paige became serious. "Tell me what happened," she said.

I stirred my spoon around in my coffee as I collected my thoughts. "Well, as you know," I began, "Both of Lexington's trials ended in a mistrial. The first was because of a hung jury, the second because of his midtrial death."

"Yes, I knew all that! How was Leonard killed?"

The impatience in her voice was evident so I rushed on not trying to sugarcoat the details. "According to the ME, whoever offed Lexington must've been mad as hell. It appeared Lexington was dispatched according to some sort of ritual. You know, the kind used in foreign countries. The ME said it looked to him like the execution was an ancient form of torture used mainly by the Chinese who believed in *inflicting death by a thousand cuts*. He also said that type of torture dated back centuries and since has been deemed inhumane and banned."

"Was that all he said?" Paige asked no longer sipping her coffee but setting it aside.

"I didn't ask for details. Just the verbiage *death by a thousand cuts* paints a pretty gruesome picture."

Paige nodded and looked away. I could only imagine what she was thinking. On the one-hand, what happened to her brother-in-law was deserved—but perhaps not to such an extreme. On the other hand, what happened to her sister was not deserved under any circumstances.

Looking at me and shaking her head, Paige murmured, "For Margot to trade her life for Leonard's political aspirations, hardly seems fair."

"Death is not a finality!" I said. "Leonard still has to account for his actions before the God of the Universe!"

• • •

On her return from her last Paris/Cairo turn,

Paige picked up her personal belongings from her landlord in Savannah and moved in with me. We discussed wedding plans and both agreed on a simple quiet wedding. However, with the pressure from our friends and relatives, our wedding turned into quite the production. I questioned the rationale behind Paige insisting we have the ceremony in the same church as Margot's funeral. She remained steadfast in her request, so I finally agreed, and it wasn't until we were exchanging vows that I understood Paige's reasoning.

"It's as though she's here spiritually if not physically," Paige whispered to me as we stood before the altar. I squeezed her hand. Her explanation made perfect sense, and as I looked at her, I reflected on how fortunate I was to have someone like Paige in my life.

After exchanging vows, we had a reception at the Denver Convention Center. Ironically, the same venue where Thornton and I arrested Lexington lo those many months ago. However, tonight was a joyful celebration and live music, dinner, and champagne toasts were the order of business. I didn't know it was possible to put the unspeakable behind us and concentrate only on a promising future. But we did and will continue to do so—God willing!

We honeymooned in Aruba, somewhere as far

from a desert, any desert, as we could get. Paige loved flying so she went to work for a domestic airline and flew out of DIA. No more foreign trips for her. I still dabble in PI work but have plenty of spare time on my hands. I'm not one to let a good story go to waste so I wrote my first novel, *Reflection of a Killer.* Although the facts were real life experiences, it was published as a work of fiction.

Today is our first wedding anniversary, and along with marking one year of marriage, we're also celebrating *Reflection of a Killer* being on the bestseller list for six-months straight.

• • •

When *Reflection of a Killer* netted five million in royalties, Paige decided to give up flying, and being financially secure for the rest of our lives, we started a family. Our four-year-old son, Jack, Jr., two-year-old daughter, Margot, and my wife Paige, needless to say, are the spice of my life. Paige's love of our nation's antebellum history prompted us to buy and remodel a Victorian in Charleston, South Carolina. The laid-back charm of the south is quite a contrast to the hustle and bustle of life in Denver and it didn't take us long to acclimate.

• • •

The downside of launching a writing career with a bestseller is that, unless you can match it, there's only one way to go. I've had the pleasure of conversing with other authors at book signings, and we agree that sales, although important, aren't the *most* important thing. It's the satisfaction of creating something worthwhile. I now spend most of my time developing plots and writing novels focusing on mystery, intrigue, and courtroom drama. I draw many scenes from my experience as a PI, and I would hope there's another bestseller in me but…only time will tell.